Me,
In Between

Me, In Between

Julya Rabinowich

TRANSLATED BY CLAIRE STOREY

ANDERSEN PRESS

First published in English in 2022 by
Andersen Press Limited
20 Vauxhall Bridge Road, London SW1V 2SA, UK
Vijverlaan 48, 3062 HL Rotterdam, Nederland
www.andersenpress.co.uk

2 4 6 8 10 9 7 5 3 1

Originally published in German as Dazwischen: Ich in 2016
by Carl Hanser Verlag, Munich

The translation of this work was supported by a grant
from the Goethe-Institut

British Library Cataloguing in Publication Data available.

ISBN 978 1 83913 124 0

Printed and bound in Great Britain
by Clays Ltd, Elcograf S.p.A.

For all the children and young people I've met
who were seeking a place to call home.

And for Naïma.

I

Where do I come from? That doesn't matter. It could be anywhere. There are many people in many countries who live through what I have lived through. I come from everywhere. I come from nowhere. Beyond the seven mountains. And much further still. A place where Ali Baba's thieves wouldn't want to live. Not any more. Too dangerous.

I have long hair. Down to my hips. I used to laugh a lot. I have a little brother and I'm not afraid of wild dogs. And I've already seen people die. So there. If you know that about me, you know more about me than most people here.

I'm just going to start with things I like. I can always come back to the things I don't like later on.

So, things I like: I like it when I hug Laura and breathe in her familiar smell. I like it when I accomplish something I've set out to do. And I like it when I can out-talk some idiot who comes my way. Because I've finally

1

mastered the language. If you stay silent, you've already lost. It's as simple as that.

I like it when the sun shines. The sky gleams a brilliant blue and if you block out the noise of the motorway, you can hear the birds singing.

Next to our house there's a tree. A large tree with dense branches where the birds sleep. I imagine they've built their nests in the knotholes of the branches. Nests like that don't fall out as easily when there's a storm. I like that even more: the idea that they're safe even when it's really windy. And the rain doesn't get in there either. Well, not much anyway.

It's a good thing really that the tree isn't right outside my window, otherwise I'd spend too much time watching the birds. Or feeding them. I often wrap up the bread rolls from breakfast and sneak them out with me so I can sprinkle the pale crumbs on our windowsill later on. You're not allowed to take food with you into the bedrooms.

Mum follows this rule to the letter. I think it's stupid.

The cook doesn't follow the rules either; she starts clearing up while we're still eating. Because of her, we all gobble our food down. Sometimes, I can barely eat anything. Sometimes, I'm just not hungry in the evening. Who's hungry at the same time every day? Not me! You can't go back for seconds, either. The best you can do is pile as much on your plate as possible. Sometimes she grumbles and then I have to hand back my bread or cheese or salami. Even if I've already touched it.

'You'll never eat all that,' she says. 'And you definitely don't eat salami. I know that much.'

I say nothing to that. Of course I can't eat that much. But I want to decide for myself when I eat and who I eat with. The birds, for instance, should always eat with me. And I give the salami to the cat in the yard before I go to school or in the evening before bed.

I've often watched the cook wrapping up our bread, salami and cheese with her precise, skilful hands. She puts it into little plastic bags from the supermarket and then into the large carrier bag she always brings with her. She comes here on a bike and sometimes the bag's so heavy that as she leaves with the bag hooked over the handlebars, she wobbles along the country lanes. My little brother Rami's so thick, he even offered her his small, colourful rucksack. Dad laughed. Rami can be such a goody two-shoes, given the chance. And since then, of course, the cook's taken a real shine to him, even slipping him some chewing gum because he comes across so well-behaved, with his big, wide eyes that Mum falls for so easily. Just like everyone else. Little brothers are pests in human form. Pests with curls.

'She's cheating us,' I said to him. 'And you really want to help her?'

'But she's so lovely,' he replied.

So of course, then I called him an idiot.

And he laughed. He thinks everybody's lovely, everybody.

Even the weirdo from the second floor, who's headbutted him a couple of times and often sticks his leg out to trip me up when I'm running down the stairs in the morning to get to the school bus.

Thing is, I'm always up on time. In summer, the birds make such a racket I'm already awake by five. But it can take up to an hour for the bathroom to become free. And waiting for my aunt to come out takes even longer. She stays in there for hours. *Hours*. Until Dad starts yelling.

There have been a couple of times when I've gone to school without a shower and spent the whole day feeling embarrassed, especially when Mona shouted out 'She stinks!' as I walked past. But perhaps she'd have said that anyway; she says it nearly every day. Luckily, not everyone laughed, and Laura didn't laugh at all.

We've made a hidey-hole for some soap in the toilets so it never happens again. In the third stall in the girls' toilets there's a loose tile on the wall. Behind it, Laura's hidden a little bar of soap, wrapped in pink paper, and I sneak out to the toilet during first period and have a wash with this little bar of soap that smells so sweetly of roses and makes me feel like I've had a bath in a whole tub of flowers.

We used to have lots of roses in our garden. And I

4

had a cat back then too. And on the way home, I'd pass a herd of goats. I like goats. Some of the farmers here keep goats. Just like my grandma.

I've not told anyone at home about it. I don't mean the goats, I mean stupid Mona's stupid name-calling. Nor have I told them about the not-washing or the rose-scented soap in the hidey-hole in the girls' toilets either, otherwise Dad might get upset again about the shower being busy, and then Mum will have to calm him down and defend her sister, Amina. And then she'll get into an argument with Amina, because my aunt really loves to argue. With everyone. But especially with Mum because she never gets angry. Either that or Mum immediately bursts into tears and then my aunt has won. I keep out of her way if I can.

If I didn't have Laura, it'd be really awful. But fortunately, she's here. I reckon I've been really lucky.

Perhaps I'll tell you about those who have been less lucky sometime.

But I don't want to do that yet.

Some people here get angry with Mum; she's often at loggerheads with them because my aunt hogs the bathroom for hours on end.

'Mrs Lema,' they begin reproachfully, 'it's not on.'

Mum placates them, talks to them, asks for compassion,

which really gets on their nerves, and given most people round here don't have many nerves left, it properly gets on their last few remaining ones. When Amina finally emerges from the bathroom, there's often an argument in the hallway. Involving several people. Amina walks straight past them without saying hello, the skin on her hands, underarms and neck glowing dark red because she's scrubbed it so hard. Sometimes I think she'll scrub her skin to shreds. She never thanks Mum. And Mum looks at her so sadly, I just want to give her a hug. Nobody says anything else. They all carry on as if it were completely normal that someone should want to tear their own skin off their body. I don't say anything either because I don't know what else to do.

2

I secretly let the cat into the room today. She curled up on my bed and purred. I lay my head next to her so I could feel her body gently vibrating. It's like the softest massage. Only without hands.

Amina says if she catches that 'fleabag' in her room again like yesterday, she'll snitch on me to the landlord, who everyone calls 'the Boss'. 'In *her* room.' Yeah, whatever.

Asked Dad whether we could stick Amina in her own room.

No, we can't. The Boss says we already have a big room. The little ones are needed for couples with babies. There aren't any single rooms here. It's not worth it.

Dad almost seems to regret it even more than me.

I don't want to be in a rubbish mood.

In a philosophical moment, Mr Bast, our biology

teacher, placed a glass of water on the desk. 'Half full or half empty?' he asked. It all depends how you look at it. Just before breaktime, he accidentally knocked it over. Whenever he's in full flow, he waves his arms about like a windmill.

I look at it like this: the glass is always half full, even if it's actually nearly empty. That's how I try to see it, anyway. But it's not really the case for us. We're not really here yet, but I'm working on it. Not that it's our decision to make, of course. But I can still try! Like when I realise I'm keeping up in just about every subject at school. That means I don't have to keep worrying about failing the year and having to repeat it while Laura passes and leaves me all on my own again. Granted, if Laura wasn't helping me, I'd already have failed a couple of assignments. Particularly in German. Maths is easier. I think the German teacher – her name's Mrs King – knows that. I think she just looks the other way. It's very kind of her. I just hope nobody else notices.

Mum's had another argument with Aunt Amina. Amina really winds people up the wrong way. Dad got involved, as always: sent Mum out and then me. Rami hid behind the wardrobe. Dad hadn't spotted him. Or didn't want to.

Mum went out into the yard and sat on the bench in the sun, holding a tissue to her eyes as if she had a cold. What else could she do – stand in the hallway with everyone walking past? The kitchen's closed in the afternoons. Women often wander around the place crying quietly. And the men argue in loud voices. Sometimes it's the women who argue loudly while the men cry, but usually only when they really are at the end of their tethers, and then other more serious things happen as well and the doctor has to be called, or the police, or sometimes both. The weirdo from the second floor was once beaten so badly by his parents he had to go to hospital. The warden wasn't bothered; it wasn't him that called the police. Don't know who did. And no sooner was the weirdo back again, he tried to have a go at Rami. Until I intervened. He may be a pest, but he's still my little brother.

I sat down next to Mum on the bench. The stripy ginger cat jumped up onto my lap, purring. I laid one hand on the soft, warm cat and the other on Mum's arm and told her funny things about school. In reality, they weren't that funny. I padded them out a bit. But I reckon that's fine in moments like that. She laughed and dabbed her eyes. I like it when she's not crying all the time.

Every morning, Dad runs down to the letterbox, as does everyone else who hasn't yet given up hope. Then he comes back silently and I know it's empty again. No decision from the authorities, no black and white decision telling us we can stay. Asylum granted. Finally. Being granted asylum is a bit like having a baby. You wait with such anticipation. The decision develops and grows, although sadly the authorities need much longer than nine months. And all the while, there's an underlying anxiety. It will change everything. Everything.

Everyone who has moved out of here received the letter first. I've seen it happen. It's either move out, get your own home or stay here. Or be picked up by the police and removed from the country. Some left straight away, others later on. Some started kicking and screaming inside the house or outside by the police car. Some police officers were kind, nearly crying themselves. Some were just brutal, enjoying it even. Almost like being back home. I couldn't look away. I stood glued to the bannisters, staring as though I was watching a horror film – you think if you look away something even worse will happen. They grabbed people by their hair. Their heads were pulled right back. I shook.

Suddenly Dad was there. I hadn't heard him. He placed his hand gently on my shoulder. 'Come, Madina,' he said. 'Come, let's go to our room. Now, come on.'

I shrank back into his arms, sinking into them, feeling his chest pressed against the back of my head. Broad and solid. I was suddenly swathed in a thick fog. Could only move with his arm across my back. Let him guide me slowly away from the bannister. Downstairs, the screams died away. He steered me carefully into our room and turned the radio up, strange music, whatever channel was on. I concentrated on the music and the female presenter's voice. So as not to hear anything else. Was so grateful to him.

'That won't happen to us,' he said. He said it so very calmly. 'Do you hear? We're staying here.'

The front door slammed and outside a car drove away.

I didn't answer. Images were running through my mind.

No, I don't want to write about that yet. Out. Stop. Now. I'm just nipping to the loo and to get a glass of water.

Right, I'm back.

Here we go again. Everyone's waiting for the letter, the one and only letter that can save you. The letter that says they're granting you asylum. In black and white. Safe. Better than just dreaming. This black and white document that means staying here. Having rights. Being a real person with a real life. And then you move out.

Three friends have already come and gone like that.

One told me she was here for nearly five years. I got to know her when we moved in. She spoke my language. That was amazing. Showed me the house, the cats, the birds. Warned me who to stay away from. Played board games with me out in the yard and told me all about the TV programmes in the common room. I couldn't speak any German then.

Two months later she'd gone. She was so happy. About the new flat. With its own kitchen and its own toilet and its own bath. Just getting into the bathroom without having to fight my aunt would be progress. We said we'd still see each other. But the new flat was in a different area, quite far away. She dropped by a few times. And then she stopped coming. I was alone again.

I don't want the same to happen with Laura. That would be awful. Laura's my oldest friend here. Since I first started school, nearly a year and a half ago. And aside from that, she's the only one who's ever come over to me just like that. Sat with me every so often. Didn't laugh at the mistakes I made in German, which everyone else, except for me, found so funny. At the beginning, I was so scared, I stuttered. That made the class laugh even more.

Sometimes I forget I had an even better friend back home. That's not right. You should never forget something like that. But then sometimes I'm really happy when I can forget Mori. In any case, I can't do anything else for her.

Or her sisters.

Mona's an even bigger pain than my little brother. I've not done anything to her.

I'd prefer to write about something nice. Something that I like. My long hair, for example. Quite a few people are envious of it, back home too. I've not cut it for about seven years at least. When I plait it, it comes right down to my waist. A beautiful, thick, shiny plait. Dad gets mad if I suggest wearing my hair down like most of the other girls at school. Laura has short, choppy hair. And Sabina – who I'm a bit jealous of because she was friends with Laura before me and who's a bit jealous of me because I get on with Laura better than she does – would never have such a boring plait. Sabina's sister is a hairdresser. Sabina's hair is quite thin and every other week she comes in with something new because her sister practises on her. Sometimes it looks good. Sometimes it's a bit OTT. And sometimes her hair's left in such a state, she has to get it cut again.

'You've got such beautiful curls,' says Sabina, who'd really like to have curls. And then she says, 'It's such a shame you tie it back all the time.'

I don't want to explain anything to her, so I tell her it's because I don't want to wear my hair down. But really, I had to fight hard to stop Dad from forcing me to wear hijab. In summer! I never wore a headscarf back home. But here, everything's different.

She picks up my plait and plays with a few loose strands at the end, making them spring up and twirling them around her fingers like a black, shiny silk ribbon. Her hair is smooth and pale like cooked spaghetti.

Sometimes the three of us go to Laura's and lock ourselves in the bathroom for almost as long as my aunt, and we try everything out: Sabina's sister's styling mousse, Laura's brother's hair gel, her mum's curlers. We're going to have a go at dyeing our hair sometime. We're dead set on it. Laura gets lots of pocket money and has already bought us some bright colours: tomato red and sea blue. Not much use for me, unfortunately; it won't show up on blue-black hair. But anyway. We put on make-up, mix face masks, and pop slices of cucumber over our eyes. We take photos of ourselves.

'Beauty immortalised,' says Laura.

Us as gorgeous women. Us as bronzed statues. Us with hot pink curlers, crimson lipstick and cats' ears. A whole album of them. I draw pretty patterns around the photos. Laura's mum loves it.

There are photos all over the walls of their home, of her, of Laura and Markus. Some of the photos have a bit cut off at the edge. One side missing. That's where Laura's dad was.

Dinner is always at seven o'clock. No earlier, no later. Quarter of an hour before the meal, everyone has to be downstairs. On the ground floor. A queue forms next to the dining room door. And then we wait. Some people get impatient, like animals in a zoo that know when it's feeding time and know that someone always comes to bring them food: meat, fish, hay and fruit. But they still get jumpy every time, as if they're not one hundred per cent certain they'll come.

At the beginning – right back at the beginning, the first few days after we arrived – we were locked up. Properly locked up. With guards in uniforms, bars on the windows and grilles across the doors and serving hatch. As if we were criminals who'd already been convicted. They looked like soldiers. Almost like the ones back home. They barked orders at us, but nobody understood. The rooms were so overcrowded. And yet they kept cramming in more and more people. Some of us had no space to sleep, so we lay on the floors in the corridors. Old people, young children, men, women.

We were all so excited because we'd made it, but overwrought at the same time. Fear made us sweat. At some point, an interpreter arrived. Looked at us disparagingly, disgusted. I've seen that look many times since. Feels like having dishwater thrown in your face.

Now when I see it, I hold my head up. And square my shoulders. Animals do that too when they want to make themselves look dangerous or important. I copy them. And I don't look away. Animals don't do that either. But it's taken a while. Firstly, to know what to do. Secondly, to be able do it.

They threw bread rolls into the room, not dished out but properly thrown, like we were in a zoo but on the wrong side of the fence. Dad always protested his case, right from the start. But still. It took them a while to believe us. And then they brought us here. It's better here. We have a dining room. The front door is always open and if we want to go outside at night and stare at the moon, we can.

3

Laura's mum gave me this diary, by the way. Just because.

'Every day you can write down what's been happening,' she said, 'I had one just like it. It's really funny when you look back on it in five or ten years' time.' She laughed. Stood there at ease in her jeans and brightly coloured trainers, leaning against the kitchen counter made from a pale wood. She looks really young, even if she is a bit chubby like Mum. Short and chubby. Behind her, blue patterned curtains, flowers and herbs in colourful ceramic pots on the windowsill. The whole place, light and airy. I love it there.

But I frowned, just fleetingly, and she didn't understand why. Perhaps she thought I didn't like her present. I really do. I just don't like the idea of writing down everything that's happened to me. The book's too nice for that.

It's covered in blue velvet, a silver lock in the middle with a dainty little key. Like in fairy tales. Only princesses have keys like that. I felt like an instant princess, an on-demand princess. But not one who's hanging about in a tower waiting for a prince. More like the sort that'll fight

17

for her kingdom. I've hung the key on my necklace together with my polished lapis lazuli pendant. The stone looks like a teardrop, a tear encased in silver. I used to wear an outstretched hand with a blue eye in the middle. Grandma gave me the lapis lazuli teardrop before we left. So I don't cry. 'So all the tears stay locked in the stone,' she'd said, while fighting back her own tears. I'll give it back when we meet again. I removed the silver palm with the blue eye from my chain and pressed it into her brown, wrinkled hand. A souvenir of me. We agreed to swap back again. Later.

I put the book under my pillow every night.

If Dad snores or Rami or my mother call out in their sleep, I bolt straight upright. And when I lurch upwards, I'm usually met with the same view: my aunt, sitting motionless by the window, staring out. Whether it's one in the morning, or three, or four. She knows I'm awake but never turns around. She says nothing. If it wasn't for the slight rise and fall of her chest, I might question if she were alive. In the moonlight, it's easier to see the movement of her throat, her chest. That's why I like it when the moon comes out from behind the clouds. I like the moon.

It happens all the time. All the time. I force myself to pretend I've not seen her and lie back down again. Reach for the velvety book cover, almost how I used to feel for my cat, back home, and then it's all OK again.

Everything in here belongs to me. And I only share it if I want to. I leave the photo album at Laura's for safety's sake. Who knows what my parents would make of it? The wild make-up and Laura's nightie. I'd prefer to be safe than sorry.

Sometimes I wake up in the middle of the night and don't know where I am. And I'm so scared I could scream. But I don't dare scream. So nobody hears me who shouldn't hear me. So nobody finds us. I feel for the light switch. I always have to sleep near the light switch. I've moved my mattress directly underneath it. Even when I touch the plastic and know I can have light at any time, it still takes a while for my heart to stop racing. And longer still until I have the courage to sit up and look around the room. Check we're all still there, where we belong. I count everyone before lying down again. Make sure nobody's missing.

I'd love to invite Laura to ours sometimes, so it's not always me going to hers after school. It makes me uncomfortable. Very. And it's pretty rude not to return the invitation. If I were at home, we'd have invited Laura over straight away. We always had guests over back then.

Mum would always cook as if there were a wedding

to celebrate, or a birthday, at least. Rice with sultanas and lamb, or chicken with plums, and salads garnished with dates and pomegranate. And that's before you start on the cakes. I really miss Mum's cakes. Not just eating them. When I was little, I was always allowed to help. It was really special, mixing the batter, the spices, rosewater and fruit. And afterwards, licking the bowls clean with Rami. Sometimes I got terrible diarrhoea from the raw batter, so did he. But we didn't care. In spring, we'd put the table outside in the garden. Cicadas chirping in the evening. And a huge full moon behind the silhouettes of the trees, the stars twinkling in the darkening night sky. Candles. There was always someone playing music. Or we'd put on a CD.

I'd love to do this just once with Laura. Even just the cake part. Licking the vanilla and cinnamon cream from the spoon with her. But I'd be even more ashamed if Laura saw how we live here. There are some really strange people in here. I'm particularly scared of one of them. He never washes, never brushes his hair, talks to himself and often calls out random things. And he follows the women around the house. There's no point in telling him not to. He just carries on. He never actually does anything. Just lurks there. But if I see him, I lock myself in the toilet until someone else needs to go.

Laura would be appalled at our toilet. Our room, too. Five mattresses on the floor and a table and four chairs, nothing else fits in the narrow room. There are never enough places for us all to sit down. Either Rami sits on Dad's lap, which if that were me, I'd find embarrassing. Or my aunt gets pushed out. Or I go, because it's all too much for me, the mood around the table, the squabbling and the squeeze.

Dad sometimes goes out for hours and nobody knows where he is. 'Walking in the woods,' he says when someone asks him. But that's not true. I've never seen him go into the woods or come out. At least not while I've been on watch in front of the house. And at the beginning, I spent a lot of time doing that. Rami says he's often seen him go down to the cellar, but never come back up again. Sometimes I'm frightened there's a secret, enchanted room into which he withdraws. It's mostly only kings and evil witches who have rooms like that. And Dad isn't either of those. He's just my dad who's sometimes too strict. But he loves me, I know that.

At the beginning, as soon as one of us was missing, we got scared. Well, perhaps not scared. But on edge. Would they come back? There are so many who haven't. The only person who always holds it together is Mum. Whatever happens, whoever's arguing and complaining. If Dad's out and it's been more than two hours, she gets nervous. She still smiles but a hard line appears on her jaw between her cheek and the corner of her mouth, reminding me of a taut bowstring from which the words she wants to say will never be shot. When I see her like this, I give her a hug. But sometimes I just want to be elsewhere.

And if I'm round at Laura's too often, Mum feels hurt and Dad gets angry.

Then my only option is to open the door to my fairy tale world and step in. I used to disappear into it back home, whenever we sat in the cellar, the plaster dust spraying down onto our heads as we counted the blasts: how close were they? How many? If there were a lot of bangs, the bombers would usually turn back because they had no more bombs on board. Mum sang songs for Rami and whenever the droning grew louder, her voice did too, as if to drown out the noise of the planes, the explosions. He buried his face firmly into her, as you would a cushion, hands over his ears. And Dad put his arms around us. Tried to hold all of us at the same time. That only ever worked if we were huddled so closely together we could no longer breathe.

I'm still not used to straying too far. I only ever wander a short distance away. And I even struggle with that.

Sometimes there's no way out but to hide inside. Then I channel all my energy to imagine. When you climb inside yourself, you can even hear the sound of birds calling in the fairy tale wood. I want colourful birds in my wood, with splendid tropical tail feathers. They aren't scared, even when the sun goes down and the shadows grow between the ancient trees.

Sometimes Dad fears I'll become as much of a stranger to him as the country that now surrounds him. But I'm sure he's just imagining that. Definitely. He's so proud of me because I can speak German well. Something he's not managed. But then he doesn't have a teacher like I do. And no Laura. He still hasn't made any friends here, unlike Mum who gets on well with four of the other women who live here. Two of them will be moving out soon, though, because they've got their papers. We don't. Perhaps Dad's scared to approach others because he hasn't got the hang of it yet. He gets much more embarrassed than I do when he makes mistakes. I think. And without me, he'd be kind of lost. That's why I often have to go with him and interpret.

Then I interpret things I don't understand. I mean, I understand the words but not the meaning. What papers he needs. Why he's here. Always the same. Really, he could just send me. On my own. Perhaps he'd enjoy that even less. But the men and women behind all the little shabby tables in all the little shabby rooms are friendlier to me than to him. I know exactly what he's going to say. I've repeated it countless times, like an organ grinder who always plays the same melody. And he gets nervous and starts sweating, and I see how annoyed he gets and has to force himself to stay calm. He succeeds most of the time. And dutifully gives the same answers time after time: why is he here? Why haven't the papers arrived yet from back home? Because our house has been bombed and is no longer standing, that's why we've brought nothing with us, and because the authorities in a country where war is raging simply don't work as efficiently and quickly as in a country where there is no war. Because Dad's on the wanted list. Not because he's committed any crime. That was the worst part, trying to convince the authorities of that. My dad is not a criminal. My dad is a medic. He would never harm anyone. Dad never wanted to harm anyone, but that alone was enough. Because in a war, it's not possible to stay out of it completely. Even when you've tried so hard. Dad quickly became a wanted man and an enemy of the state, so quickly he didn't see it coming.

'Aha!' say the officials sat at all the shabby little tables in all the shabby little rooms. 'So he was just doing his job. Then why is his life in danger?'

And I start right back at the beginning: how badly injured people would be laid at our door. How Dad clearly couldn't just let them die on our doorstep. Even if they were rebels.

'Aha!' they say. 'So you were actively supporting the perpetrators?'

Dad's patients. The resistance fighters and the regime supporters. Or in other words: the rebels and the soldiers. It was always the same. Only the names changed. The names change but the violence remains. You just can't run fast enough. Whatever you're running away from is already there, lying in wait. Like an eagle and a hare. A mean trick. But nobody here knows it. I have to explain that first. And then Dad gets cross and says we'd have all been killed anyway had he refused to help. By one side if he helped or the other side if he didn't. And not helping at all would have been even worse.

They ask him – well, me, because I'm interpreting – why he can't prove I'm his daughter. Perhaps I'm actually someone else.

I simply don't understand why they don't believe us. You can tell I'm his daughter. I look just like him. I've often shown them: our hands are exactly the same, the thumbs, the fingers, even the shape of our nails. Why would I pretend to be his daughter? That's crazy.

4

I asked Dad when we can invite guests over again. How long we'll be here for. I want to leave.

'We'll celebrate when we're allowed out of here,' he said. And then he added, 'You just have to wait.'

'I can't wait any more,' I replied.

And he said, 'Then you need to learn how. Keep trying, every day.'

Every day Dad waits for us to be allowed to move out. But it's taking ages.

Everybody here's waiting. There's nothing else to do. Until the starting pistol goes. This waiting is weightless, like objects in space. No ground. No up, no down. The adults float around in circles because there's simply nothing else for them to do. Those who are still minors have it easier. We're allowed something. We do something. The adults float in orbit and we're comets, pulled this way and that by school and nursery and the great wait. That helps.

The stamp that will be thumped onto Dad's paper is the Big Bang, from which the here and now of a new universe is created. Only then does time begin.

Those who have given up waiting either grow very quiet, hardly leaving their rooms. Or they begin to erupt. I've learned to get out of their way. When they rage long and hard, they get taken away. I don't know where they go. I don't want to know either.

We're never going there.

The weirdo has told Rami about his computer game. Rami hangs around with him quite a lot, up on the top floor. He's never played, just listens, ears burning. It's about an assassin who climbs up buildings and towers and seems mainly interested in killing people. Rami pulled a poster out the bin and stuck it on the wall in our room. Now he's demanding I call him Altair. I don't think so! But Mum's actually doing it. I asked her whether she realised she's giving her son a killer's name. She said it's a good, traditional name. I showed her the poster. She looked blankly at it. Then started calling Rami Rami again. But still lets him play assassins, springing out at me from behind corners and making my aunt jump when she's in the bathroom. I'm just waiting for Amina to get fed up. She's three times as chilling as his assassin.

Had to move really quickly on the way to the school bus today. The creep who follows the women around the house tried to intercept me on the ground floor. I didn't turn around. The whole corridor reeked of him. He looks like he came straight from hell. Unshaven, stinking, his hair matted and sticking out. Sometimes he howls in the night like an animal. He'd definitely be the sort of thing that emerges from the ground in a graveyard. I'd banish him from my fairy tale wood if his revolting head ever appeared between the tree roots. I'd scare him off with a flare.

Yesterday, he spent the whole day standing at the bottom of the stairs, gawping at everyone who went past. The women, sickeningly. The men, hatefully. He had his hands in his trouser pockets the whole time, like he was hiding something. Some of the men sped up as they walked past, even those who are usually quick to make a scene. Some stuck their hands in their pockets, like a mirror image, making out they too had something in there. Watch out!

He stared at Mum's bottom. Grinning. She didn't notice. She was carrying two heavy buckets of dirty water and was watching her every step so as not to spill any. Wobbled her way along as if on a tightrope, so carefully. Sometimes, Mrs Boss – the landlord's wife – lets us do small jobs for money. Everyone fights for it. A bit of lawn mowing or stair cleaning. Dad wasn't there. Just me. I pressed myself up behind Mum. Didn't want his gaze to fall on my back, legs or bum. Like the dirty water on the asphalt in the yard.

We're having pizza at Laura's tomorrow. I love pizza. Homemade, the whole baking tray full, covered with whatever her mum can think of: anchovies, capers, vegetables. Piles of cheese on top, cooked until it's beautifully crispy. The baking tray on a heat-pad comes to the huge wooden table. Exquisite plates of painted china. Laura's mum painted them herself. Each plate different. With names on the underside: one for Laura, one for her older brother.

Before, when Laura and Markus were little, they had plates with animals in the middle to motivate them to eat up. Laura had a cat because of her green eyes. Laura's mum showed me the old children's plates, probably because she's proud of her painting. Markus really didn't want her to. He blushed. I thought that was quite sweet.

Sometimes I go home with them after school. I know there's always a plate for me and I can always sit and eat with them. She's said she might even paint one for me. That'd be nice. Not just any plate, but *my* plate.

'You're weird,' Laura said. 'That's just for little kids.'

I don't care. I'd still like it.

Sometimes Laura's mum drops me back later on. By car, so I don't have to walk. It takes a while. Straight through the wood. During the day I enjoy walking through it. When it's dark though, ten horses couldn't drag me. Not even if Laura was there with me.

Firstly, I'd still be scared, even if she came with me.

29

Secondly, I'd then be worried about her because she'd have to go back alone. I know it's just a harmless stretch of woodland and no angry, armed people are going to spring out at me on the path, but it doesn't help. Just knowing doesn't help. Laura laughs and reassures me she's walked this stretch since she was seven and nothing has ever happened, but that doesn't help either. She taps me lightly on the forehead and laughs. When she laughs, her nose crinkles. It's really cute, like a little mouse snuffling. She has a sprinkling of freckles across her nose. Against her pale skin, they look really cute, too.

All my head can feel is the fear. This fear is so firmly lodged in there that sometimes I just want to shake it violently, or hit it really hard, not gently like Laura. And catapult out this ridiculous feeling, like the brightly coloured pills I stuck up my nose as a child and then couldn't get out again. First my father lifted me up by the legs and shook me, a pointless thing to do, and then he dripped water into my nostrils. That only made me think I was suddenly drowning; it didn't help at all. In the end, he smacked me on the back of the head with the palm of his hand until they flew out. After that, at least Rami never dared to stick anything up his nose. But still.

Today I went for a walk with Dad. For a 'serious talk'. Thought it'd be really boring. But no. Sometimes you deceive yourself. Made ourselves sandwiches and took them with us. Water bottles in the rucksack. And off we went. Straight through the wood. Climbed up a mountain. Halfway up I wanted to stop, but Dad insisted we keep going.

'Wait until you're really tired,' he said. 'Then you can stop and rest. But don't forget, that isn't the point where you turn around. It's just the point where you summon all your strength. Only then does the real path begin. Have you noticed that?'

We sat on a fallen, moss-covered tree trunk. My feet didn't reach the ground, it was so wide. A rook called the alarm, warning the others about us. We looked out over the fir trees below us, the clouds floating briskly above us. The wind was fresh. Pleasantly cool. Cool enough to sharpen the senses and make you alert, every muscle tensed. Not sleepy like you feel in a heatwave, even if you do want to be outside.

'Of course,' I said.

'OK. Tell me when you have enough energy and we'll keep going.'

'Do we really need to go all the way up?' I moaned. 'My shoes are rubbing. I don't want to any more.'

'Yes, we do,' he said.

We carried on. We filled the empty water bottles in a stream that crossed our path.

'I want you to know how to achieve your goals,' he said.

'I know that already.'

'Not well enough.' And he sped up.

I panted behind him. I was so angry. With myself because I was exhausted already and with him because he didn't glance back at all.

'I want to go back.'

'You'll enjoy the view when we get to the top. Come on.' And we kept going.

I stumbled up a steep section and grazed my knee. He cleaned the wound and we carried on.

'Tired?' he asked after a while.

'I can't feel my feet any more,' I replied.

'You can wear them out even more then.' And he turned around, saw the expression on my face. Smiled. 'Save the energy you're wasting on anger and use it for walking.'

We walked and walked. The pain faded into the background. You get used to it. I don't know how we walked for days on end. Nights on end. And every time one of us began to flag, Dad quietly but firmly insisted we keep going. He carried Rami time and time again. Once, I'd wanted to put the rucksack down. No. Not allowed. Blisters on my feet. And then, no more plasters. I still have the scars. I left my jacket behind in a wood while we were resting. We couldn't go back. Dad gave me his jumper. Said he never got cold. I believed him because I had to believe him. Otherwise I could never have taken his jumper. Behind us lay fire and gunshots. The further away we got, the quieter it became.

'Nobody gives up,' Dad said. 'Nobody stays behind. We leave together. We arrive together.'

I would walk differently. Lighter, slower, more intuitively. I'd retreat into my fairy tale wood, the place I always go when it's all too much, when I can't take it any more. I'd close my eyes and be instantly transported. I'd marvel at the scenery and the constellations above me. I'd be guided by the stars. On my journey, I'd walk mostly at night. Huge, broad trees like the ones in my picture books.

My wood is a wood where you'd find fairies and dragons, griffins and other fantastic creatures. I used to love reading fairy tales. About cannibals and wizards, talking horses and enchanted meadows. About damsels looking after bewitched, sleeping princes. For seven long years. And then, seven years later, he decides to marry another; not the girl who'd stayed by his side. Here they have different fairy tales. Laura's lent me her books. To practice my German. Here there are fairy tales about glass coffins and royal frogs and about girls wearing red shoes, who have to dance on a piece of bread for all eternity. And angry wolves.

I've actually seen wolves. There were wolves in the forests we travelled through to get here. Not everyone made it through the forests. When we lit a fire and made lots of noise, the wolves stayed back in the shadows. You could only see their eyes glinting. Lots of them. I'd give myself a firm talking-to, telling myself they were just cats' eyes.

I've never seen wolves in the woods here. Not even large dogs.

After the forests, large numbers of us traipsed through the rain. Sometimes through fields. In front of us, some people had collapsed. Some were dragged along on bedsheets. Some stayed lying where they were. Dad couldn't carry anyone else other than Rami. He tried. But he just didn't have the energy. Sometimes he wakes up yelling that he can carry someone else. He'll try to anyway, he calls. Then Mum strokes his face and coos, 'Shhhhh, it's over now. It's all over.' But it still takes several minutes for him to stop shouting.

We crossed borders with barbed wire. We lifted it up and crawled under, as quickly as possible. Once I got caught on it and scratched my back. Dad still had some disinfectant. That was good. Other people's wounds became infected. Sometimes there were soldiers. Some were friendly and gave us food and drink. Others hunted us. Then people ran around like headless chickens, shouting and chaos all around. 'Don't lose sight of me!' Mum shouted. 'Stick close to me! Hold on to me!'

High up, I was so engrossed in my thoughts that I barely noticed the summit before us. The clouds rolled back and a ray of sunlight broke through. The gusts of wind grew stronger. I pulled up my hood. Turned around. Beneath us, the wind shook the trees. We were standing in a meadow. The grass moving like waves, like a vast green ocean, patterns forming and fading away again. At the crest of the mountain stood a large iron cross.

I'd made it again. Thanks to Dad. He proves to me over and over that if I really want something, I can achieve it. That's a pretty cool thing to know. I just always forget it.

'We're there,' Dad said, putting his arm around my shoulders and pulling me close. I let him, pressing my cheek against his prickly sweater. I love this Dad-smell. When I was little, it was always the same. And still is. Only the smell of tobacco has gone because Dad doesn't smoke any more. Mum's very pleased about that.

We stood on the very top of the mountain. Just us two. We could see down into the valley beneath. The streets in the village snaking between the yellow and green fields. The swimming lake. The grey roof of the supermarket. On the other side rose a mountain higher than ours, its summit naked and barren, nothing green, just huge boulders. Above its peak, dark clouds rolled and heaved like an ogre roaming across the sky. From deep in its bowels came a rumble. A blue-grey dragon, whose belly lit up now and then. You couldn't hear any thunder yet. Only birdcall, the wind rustling in the trees.

'Don't be scared,' said Dad. 'It'll blow over.'

By the way, I have a massive craving for fruit and ice cream. It strikes me that I keep writing about food. I'm not really as greedy as it sounds. But when you only ever get the same thing every day, and every day it's just as disgusting as the day before, and the day before that, you never really get used to it. Quite the opposite. Your thoughts constantly revolve around what you'd really like. To be honest, that's really what Mum's been doing half her life because she refuses to get fat and is always on a diet. She never takes pleasure in what she really fancies, all just to try and look like my aunt.

It's a futile exercise, really. My aunt is tall and thin, on the verge of skinny and wiry, because she's barely eaten anything since we got here. But not to lose weight; she has no need for that. And it's not like her at all; she used to be properly beautiful. She'd never leave the house without her black eyeliner or her curved eyebrows. Now she never puts make-up on. Her cheeks are hollow, dark shadows under her eyes, wrinkles around her mouth. I look more like Dad, who looks like Grandpa, while Mum looks more like her mother. Amina was so pretty that everyone wanted to marry her. And she made sure Mum knew it. Mum has never forgotten.

I think Mum is much prettier. But that doesn't help. People close to you appear more beautiful than strangers.

And of course, Mum thinks Rami is the most beautiful child on God's earth because he is her only son. As I've already said, I think he's a little pest. He'll be starting school soon, then I really won't hold back any more. Then he'll be big enough to take it.

5

Laura's mum wanted to bring a whole bagful of stuff down to the hostel for us yesterday. Things belonging to Laura, her and her ex-husband. She's still got loads of stuff he never collected. 'The time has come,' she said. 'I'm getting rid of all the old junk. New times are beginning.' She laughed.

She laughs a lot; loud and infectious. My mother would never do that. With her mouth wide open. Like Laura and me. I think she's much younger than Mum. While she's cooking, she listens to music, dances and drinks wine. Sometimes we dance with her. We clear up and turn on the dishwasher. 'A dishwasher is the crowning glory in the kitchen,' she says. After our family parties, I used to stand with Mum for hours on end, washing up by hand until the skin on our fingertips turned soft, while Rami sat with the men outside. Back then, I didn't have a problem with it. I do now. My grandmother used to call wrinkly white fingertips 'lion paws'.

I hope we'll get a dishwasher soon, too. I hate washing up. All Laura has to do is load and unload the pots. Same goes for her brother Markus. He doesn't usually arrive until later on. I've not seen much of him. Looks like Laura. Freckles and reddish hair. He's tall and thin. 'A bean pole,' says Laura. He always gets grumpy at that. When she says it in front of me, anyway. I don't dare talk to him. If he's there any earlier, I leave. I have to be home by seven p.m. anyway. His things must have been in the bag as well. But they wouldn't have fitted Rami or Dad.

'Well, give them to anyone else you live with,' Markus had suggested. 'I'm not going to wear them any more.'

Told Laura's mum we didn't need anything. I really don't want her to see everything here. My father would be ashamed. His shoes are already worn out. That's another reason why he's ashamed. He doesn't say anything, but I know. Mum's already sewn the fabric up twice where his toes press against the shoe; it just keeps splitting open.

Rami has it good. He keeps growing out of everything, but so do all the other kids here and then he gets the hand-me-downs that are too small for them. Sometimes it's just tough luck though. He had to go around wearing pink trainers because there were only girls' winter shoes to pass on. He howled. And I tried colouring in the trainers with a black permanent marker. Of course, the ink then ran. And he spent the whole spring with black feet and toes. After we washed them, they turned grey. The marker really was permanent. Mum moaned. I was only trying to help. And Rami had said it was better to

39

have black feet than be a girl. Dad defended me. And that was the end of the shoe discussion.

Until the landlady stuck her nose in.

'Go and wash,' Mrs Boss said to Rami. 'Here, everyone is clean.'

This is the same person we constantly have to argue with to get a new bar of soap because she'd prefer to forget. And sometimes, toilet paper, too.

My mother turned bright red. And I could tell my father wanted to say something, probably even shout it, but he couldn't say anything, couldn't defend Rami. Nobody wants trouble here. Then they'd forget to pay us the allowance we're given every weekend. And we'd be powerless to prove it. Those that do complain get forgotten about the next time, too.

That all happened last year. Rami was younger then. I don't think he'd have any of it this year. He'd probably prefer to run around barefoot. And then he'd have black feet anyway.

Yesterday Laura overslept and arrived late to school. Two whole hours. Looked confused. Quite confused anyway.

'What's wrong?' I asked her.

'I'll get us some drinks,' Laura said.

So we went to the vending machine in the foyer, took out the bottles that fell with a loud thump into the tray below. Laura didn't wait, opened her bottle immediately. Coke sprayed in a brown fountain, sprinkling her white T-shirt. I tried not to laugh, but I had to; so did she. We were still laughing as we reached the playground and sat down. Laura had red blotches on her face and brown ones on her shirt. Unique. Very unique.

We drank the coke in small sips so neither of us finished before the other. And still Laura said nothing. Breaktime was nearly over. And I was getting more and more curious. If you can call that uneasy feeling curiosity. When I get the feeling something's changed, that something unexpected is happening, I prefer to presume it's something bad.

'Come on,' I said. 'Tell me!'

'I met Christian yesterday evening,' said Laura, blushing even redder.

Christian who? I thought. I didn't know any Christians in school, but then I don't know everyone.

'The friend of a friend of Markus's.'

This friend of a friend of Markus's must be absolutely amazing, judging by the look on her face, anyway. She was glowing from the tip of her chin all the way up to the top of her forehead; I could even see the red glowing through her pale fringe.

'It was really just an accident,' she assured me. 'Pure accident. I was at the petrol station because Mum had forgotten the milk. He helps out there.'

The bell rang, break was over. Reluctantly we stood up. It was obvious I was going to get a whole heap of notes during next lesson. I felt Laura's excitement spreading to me. And I hadn't even seen Christian, this friend of a friend of Markus's.

Next class was biology. Cell division. Our biology teacher, Mr Bast, is so young. He really has no idea yet. Sometimes he just lets us walk all over him. Gossiping in class, for example, just because he wants to look cool. But shortly before exams, he starts panicking and expects absolute obedience and attention to work. Unfortunately, we were now at the start of June, the final throes of exam term, and he was being really strict and demanding, threatening minus grades and report cards.

I scribbled Laura a note with just a large question mark on it and pushed it carefully towards her with my biology book. Laura was still glowing, as if she were a rocket or a comet and had just entered the atmosphere of an unknown planet. She stared at the piece of paper and didn't answer straight away. I leafed through the book, glancing at Laura and then back at the book, and then suddenly Mr Bast was standing next to me, his eyebrows raised. No sooner had he walked past, I flicked away from cell division. To people and their bodily functions. So far, I'd managed to purposefully avoid it. I quickly opened and closed the most embarrassing pages. Laura peered across at me.

'It's ridiculous,' she whispered. 'I only walked with him as far as our house. I was so nervous, I picked off half of Mum's lilacs while we stood at the front door. Oh my God.'

'You stood outside your house?'

'Yes, but not for long.'

Long enough to pick off half of your mum's lilacs though, I thought.

'I told him I was scared of the dark.'

'*You?*'

'Yeah, I got that idea from you.'

That's really not funny, Laura, I thought. But I didn't say anything. I thumped my biology book closed and pretended to listen really hard to Mr Bast.

I can never stay cross with Laura for long. After half a day, I start to miss her. I gobbled down my breakfast to get to the bus, that, and because Rami was being annoying and pulling my hair. Mum gave me a kiss. I'm going to try and talk to Laura about Christian again today. There's something about the whole thing that makes me feel uncomfortable. But I'm really not sure what it is. It's strange. Perhaps I just don't want to share her.

I went to the letter box today instead of Dad. Still nothing. He didn't ask; he was watching me.

Went for a walk with Mum in the wood. We collected a pile of wild strawberries and added them to our glasses of milk during dinner. Tastes better than milkshake. Rami's milk intolerant so he's going to have tummy ache, greedy thing. But it won't be me running to the toilet with him in the middle of the night. I've made that very clear.

Oh, great. At three in the morning he came over to me. 'I don't feel very well.'

I didn't want to wake up; I have to leave for school really early and waking in the night makes me so tired. 'Be quiet,' I grumbled, pushing him away.

He sat down on my mattress. 'But I feel really sick.'

'Then go to Mum,' I said, but it was too late. He threw up all over my bed. And I didn't get any clean bedding until morning. Everything smelt sour. We all had to get up. Mum gave me her blanket. I'd have thrown up myself if I'd have had to lie down again with that Rami-sick smell.

If Laura only knew what this place looked like. This place where we sit, hour after hour, waiting until our names are finally called ... Linoleum-lined corridors, flickering florescent striplights. When you have to spend the whole day here, everyone ends up in a bad mood. It's the narrowness, the harsh lighting, the bad odours. It smells of angst-ridden sweat and fatigue, of anger and impotence. There's usually a water fountain in the corner of the waiting room. Often there are no cups left. Because so many people come here, every day, to sit in front of the different doors. The toilets stink. Some people just pee on the floor. The men because they're careless and the women because they're scared of sitting on the toilet seat, instead trying to hover, balancing over the bowl. The better-equipped buildings have numbered tickets you pull out of a machine. Everyone holds a piece of paper with their number. All the numbers will eventually be called out. Eventually. Where there are no numbers, there's always someone who'll try to push in. And if you start to argue with them, half the time they go in front anyway because they just make more noise, and the staff are either too indifferent or too tired to bother policing it. I can't imagine it's much fun for them either, spending eight hours a day in such a small box being shouted at or cried on for about five of those hours. Really not fun. Some of them are actually still really nice. Others just don't care.

Sometimes we get letters from Grandma. When that happens, Dad's still disappointed it's not our asylum decision, but is a little brighter than when we get absolutely nothing. Grandma doesn't write very often because she can't see very well. Sometimes she dictates to Uncle Miro, Dad's younger brother. Then the letter is easier to read.

Her hand shakes as she writes and you have to guess every word. Dad reads the letters and sighs. Rubs his chest near his heart. She only writes nice things, but that never reassures him. What the goats are doing. And the hens. What the lambs have been up to this time. One even got into the kitchen and tried to eat the flowery tablecloth. It knocked everything off the table and fled to the garden at the sound of the vase shattering on the floor. It was difficult to catch the trembling animal again.

Rami listens and laughs himself silly. Then he gets bored and runs off. I stay, on my own, to comfort Dad. He reads again and again, getting quieter and quieter. Grandma writes about which neighbours she's visited. What she's cooked for Grandpa. What the weather is like. She never writes about the war, as if it simply wasn't happening any more, as if we could just go back. Anytime.

Mum makes tea for us in the little kitchen, carrying it up several flights of stairs. Gives Dad one more sugar lump than usual and goes without one for herself.

'The tea's good,' Dad always says. 'Thanks.'

And then he lets it go cold.

Today there's a big fair down in the village. Laura wanted me to go with her. No chance. Of course, Dad wouldn't let me go. As with the seven previous invitations I had to turn down, there are no exceptions. The others are going to eat chips, ride the bumper cars, listen to music. I'm missing it all.

This morning I watched them put up the stands. The market stalls. I didn't argue with Dad; there was no point. Was sad. But for once, not so sad. Watched some TV in the common room, then was tired and went to bed early. So I didn't have to think about what Laura was doing at the fair. Whether that boy Christian was there, or Sabina.

It's uncomfortably warm tonight, the sky cloudless. Before I go to sleep, I gaze at the stars. Look for and find the Big Dipper, what we call the Great She-bear. I've done this before bed since I was little. Out in the garden, looking for the constellations with Mum. So the She-bear will watch over me as I sleep. Wish the Great She-bear good night. Lie down next to Rami. As always, Mum and Dad leave the room until he is fast asleep and they can come back in. In summer, they can go for a walk or sit in the yard, that's not so bad. The yard is peacefully quiet now. The landlords aren't there; they've gone to the fair, dressed up like they're going to a wedding. I curl up under the blanket. Hear Rami's childlike snores, such a calming, snuffling sound, listen to him for a while, thinking about where my aunt is: I haven't seen her all day.

In the middle of the night, all hell breaks loose. I wake up because someone is screaming dreadfully. Sickeningly. So loud and piercing it gives you goosebumps. Like chalk on a blackboard, makes your teeth hurt. At first, I don't know where I am. I need a moment to work out I'm not in bed but in the corner of the room. As far from the window as possible, cowering, my arms wrapped around me so tightly that the next day I'm covered with red marks and bruises. Later, I realise it was me who had been screaming.

Outside the sky glows red. I'm terrified because I don't understand what has happened, why I'm sitting in the corner and not in bed. The next ear-splitting bang. And a ball of exploding light amongst the softly twinkling stars; first red, then fading to a white and yellow rain, another bang and a green shower of sparks. Smoke blows sideways, smells like gunpowder, smells like gunshot, smells like so many of my nights had smelled, feels how those nights had felt.

I scream and scream, and Dad tears open the door and runs to me and tries to lift me up, and I scream louder still and push him away with all my might. Somewhere in the background, Rami howls. He howled like that back home, too. Everything is just like it was, everything. 'It's just a firework, a firework,' roars Dad as he holds me in a bear hug that I cannot escape from, ignores me kicking his shins. 'It's OK, Madina! Just a firework!' He lifts me up and hugs me so tight our bones knock against each other. I feel his hands on my shoulders, and then nothing else.

I've gone.

I'm there again.

I'm on the road in front of the little grocery store belonging to Mori's father, feeling the heat of the hot street, hearing the hum of the insects that circle above the fruit that Mori's mother has put on the small wooden bench for us so we can enjoy a snack when we finish playing.

Mori laughs, carrying her little sister who she has to look after. Lolo. With blue eyes and fair curls, arms still round and chubby, so chubby she has funny creases between her wrists and hands. Lolo laughs, too; only has a couple of small teeth in her mouth. Sparkling tiny white teeth, like a little animal. We skip around, once, twice, holding hands. Mori's mother comes out of the house carrying a blue jug filled with weak juice, and as she goes to set it down on the bench next to the apples and figs, there's suddenly such a loud bang that several days later I still can't hear out of my left ear. There's a bang and I don't know where I am. I see Mori's house pass me by at a very strange angle, then just grass all around me, grass sprinkled with red.

Lift my hand. The hand is also sprinkled with red. I don't understand anything. I stand up, the sand is full of red puddles. People come running; others, knocked over by the impact of the explosion, lying at the edges of the road, get up dazed and shout something or nothing at all. Mori's father. Mori's mother. Someone lifts me up. Someone takes me away.

'Where's Mori?' I whisper. While they carry me, out of the corner of my eye, I see people-sized dolls in the road wearing charred clothing, singed hair sticking strangely out of their heads like straw. Puppets, scarecrows, I think. Not people. Not people. They're not people.

Then my father slaps my face. Really hard. My cheek burns. That brings me back. I reach for my tingling skin, feel my hand again, feel my face, my gaze widens a little, I see our room again. Mum stands with Rami in the doorway, her large round eyes frightened, standing there like an oversized owl. Blinking. Rami's screaming his little heart out.

'Has Madina gone crazy?' he howls. 'Has she gone mad?'

Dad brings a glass to my lips.

'Drink,' he says. 'Drink it.'

I place my dry lips over the edge of the glass and let the liquid run down my throat. The water tastes bitter. It tastes funny.

'Good,' he says. 'Good.'

And he lays one hand over my eyes and continues holding me tight with the other, pushing me towards the mattress. I struggle a little but become soft and limp as if my limbs no longer belong to me. Just as he'd done back home. Exactly the same. When someone lay injured at our front door. When we tended their wounds. They lay in our cellar, sometimes as many as five at a time; Mum and I cooked for them, and Dad looked after the injuries. Some made it. Others didn't. We buried them with all the rituals behind our house. The cemetery had been bombed long before.

We boiled bloody bandages; we asked the neighbours for medicine.

A real little field hospital.

Good that Dad knew how. Good that he had been a medic before. Bad, though, that we weren't really allowed to help the injured. We had to do it in secret, hidden. Later, someone wrote *Traitor to the people* on our house. But if we hadn't helped them, Dad said, the other side would've killed us. When it's war, there are always at least two sides, and if you're in the middle, there aren't many options left. Even I know that. Now.

It's good that Laura doesn't know about it. Let her enjoy her Christian and the summer nights and the dark alleyways with lilacs.

Didn't go to school today. Watched the legs of my parents and my aunt walking around our table. Haven't said a word. Didn't want to. Couldn't either. Mum brought my food to the room. I didn't touch it. Perhaps Laura called. Perhaps not. Nobody's said anything. Rami isn't here, they've sent him to the neighbours. To play.

Rami draws tanks and fighter jets. With pencil crayons and enthusiasm. 'If you're brave, you fight,' he says. 'And if you fight, you win.'

'Rubbish,' I say.

'No, it's not,' he replies. 'If you don't fight, then you're a loser. That's what *he* said upstairs.'

'He talks a lot when there's nothing else to do, Rami. He's a dick.'

I know he was so scared he cried when the Boss had a go at him about a ball that had gone flying through a window. I know that much. Snot and tears, that's what he cried, our hero from the second floor.

Sometimes I think I'll never be like I was before. And then I ask myself: what was I like back then? Sometimes I can't even remember any more. Don't think I used to laugh much then either, or maybe I did. It's all so blurry. Only laugh occasionally now.

I'm confused. My insides are like a ball of wool that someone has unwound and then wound back up again really badly. Perhaps even just crumpled it all together, as though this heap of spaghetti yarn were a ball. Pressed it all together, deceiving anyone that doesn't look too closely. But I won't let myself be deceived.

I want to go to Grandma. In moments like these she always knows what to do. She takes me in her arms. She smells of spices, mingled with the slight odour of sweat. But I like it, that's how grandmas are meant to smell. So much work, so much cooking leaves its trace. That's OK. When I'm old and I hug my grandchildren, I won't smell of roses either. Her skin is wrinkly and soft, like the saggy bellies of old cats. Brown-tanned face and hands, milk-white everywhere her clothes cover. But in her bedroom, she takes off her apron, the colourful dresses and her overcoat, and her throat emerges from the top of her flowery nightie, pale and slender like a crescent moon. Surrounded by a colourful sea of roses. I lean into her, snuggle my cheek into the crescent, and she rubs my shoulders, lightly, forwards and backwards, like she used to stroke our cats, and our goats. If I were there now, I'm sure I'd tell her everything, say everything I need to say, be able to cry. Because the unspoken words are stuck in my throat, taking my air. Words like chicken bones.

Mum sits down next to me, hugs me. No smell of sweat, or spices. Just a hint of household soap, the one Mrs Boss has finally put in the bathroom. But she says nothing. Almost in tears herself. So I can't say anything then. Don't want to make her even sadder; I feel sorry for her but I'm angry at the same time. Then I imagine sneaking out of the house in the middle of the night, past the watchful eyes of my aunt as she stares at the moon, my mother's quiet breathing, me, stealing out, turning at the doorway, a last glance back at everyone: Dad, his hair and beard ruffled, his arm around Mum, her lying with her head on his chest, which is almost as hairy as his head. At his temples he's almost completely white, a sprinkling of grey around the sides, but on top his hair is as jet-black as mine. When I'm in a good mood, I call him a chipmunk. When he's in a good mood, I'm allowed.

'Chipmunk Daddy,' I say in my daydream. 'Sleep well, Mum,' I say. And then, 'Be good, Rami.'

And then I press the door handle down, slowly so it doesn't make a noise, and open the door in slow motion. Listen again, check Rami's still breathing deeply and quietly. And step through it, leaving the door open so it doesn't slam, and run down the stairs, past all the rooms, through the main entrance, tiptoe across the yard, past the dog houses on the left-hand side near the landlords' home, making sure I don't step on any twigs or branches, nothing that could crack. Creep through the wood in the moonlight. Goodbye. Farewell, Laura. I don't turn around. If I did, my eyes would meet my aunt's stony gaze. I don't ever turn around and I keep going, day and night, travelling over the sea, at night lying on my back on the top deck of a ship, staring into space, looking out for the Great She-bear. Another time, I'll explain where the journey's heading. But it's really quite easy to guess.

6

Feeling better today. Still not been to school though.
Laura hasn't called.

Laura's still not called. Today's Saturday.

Sunday is so boring. It's raining. Everyone's stuck inside
and getting on each other's nerves. No nursery, no school,
no German classes. The men have taken over the TV and
are watching football. I'll be happy when the weekend's
over.

I miss Laura. But I wonder why she's not been in
touch. Makes me nervous.

Dreamed about Mori last night. About her sister. We
smiled at each other; they were standing on the other side
of the road. Mori was wearing her red dress with the blue
embroidery around the hem, wearing her new shoes her

uncle had brought for her from the city, the ones she was so proud of. I wasn't even allowed to touch them. Black ballerina pumps with a narrow leather strap. She was holding her little sister's hand to stop her running into the road. Cars kept going past, blowing up clouds of dust. It was early morning. The sun wasn't yet high in the sky and we cast long shadows into the red sand, like mythical figures. They stood on the other side of the road and waved at me, frantically at first, and then less so because I didn't react straight away. I just stared at them, and then slowly raised my hand because I knew something wasn't quite right, something seemed odd. But at the same time, I was so pleased to see them again. Then I laughed. Waved. Wanted to run across to the other side, hug Mori, breathe in the smell of her hair, she has incredibly soft skin on her neck. Had to watch out for cars though. A lorry drove past, as long as a train, on and on, and as it was passing, I realised that no lorry in the world is as long as a train and that I must be dreaming. I woke up.

As I opened my eyes, I could still feel the cosy warmth of friendship in my belly. I stared at the ceiling in our room and after lying still for a while and looking up, I spotted a tiny black spider hanging helplessly in the room, her cobweb in the first stages of construction.

Then I thought, 'But you're both dead.'

Sometimes I'd like to talk to Laura about it. Tell her I'm cheating on Mori with her. That every day I learned, joked, played and ate with Mori. That I'm pushing her, Laura, over the top of Mori so I don't have to see her any more. So there's something new for me.

Nobody can ever replace someone else, as if they'd never existed. But my time is moving on and Mori's is standing still. My time is pushing me onwards, pushing me further and further away, until Mori is no longer a part of my day-to-day, but is something I have to make an effort to remember. I can no longer decide whether she had light or dark brown eyes. Sometimes I ask myself questions. What was her second youngest sister called? What did we do during the holidays five years ago? I'm not so sure any more. I mean, I'm not so sure about my Mori-past any more. I look back and it all looks the same until the colours begin to fade. And sometimes I'm pleased it's fading. Then I feel ashamed. It's not fair. It's just not fair. If I forget her, it's like she was never there. Here Mori only exists in my memory. Mum perhaps still knows a bit about her. Rami doesn't remember anything any more. Or he pretends not to because he doesn't want to remember. And the little ones simply forget quicker.

When I was four years old, I had a cat. She got run over. Not intentionally; it was one of Dad's friends. He just didn't see her and crushed her while he was parking outside our house. Even so, he brought her in to us. It was too late. She bled so much a thin red line dripped along the gravel path in front of our house, from his car to the front door. I cried for days. But then I forgot about the cat, and after that, the thin red line. Later on, we got another cat and I didn't think about the first one at all. I reckon that's how it'll be with Rami. He has new friends here. He doesn't think of the friends back home. Nor our grandparents, nor our uncle. Nor the neighbours.

I still remember the house above them collapsing. I was older by then. The taste of dust on my tongue, sand between my toes. And the fear that you weren't only breathing in dust, but particles of what had once been our neighbours. All mixed in together. Inhaling the neighbours and preserving them in your lungs, absorbing them into your bloodstream. I couldn't sleep for days; I was so scared they were now stored somewhere in my body.

Sometimes during the night, ridiculous thoughts would cross my mind: whether people who have been murdered could penetrate a different body and control it, possessing me or poisoning me because they were jealous that their house was destroyed while ours survived repeated bombings, as if by magic, while the buildings on either side went up in flames. Some people even whispered that Mum was a witch. She didn't dare to laugh at them. I didn't dare to share my thoughts with her about inhaling the neighbours. At some point, Grandma realised I wasn't sleeping at night, sat down next to me, put her arms around me and sang to me. I told her about it. On the fourth night. She smiled and said the neighbours were now my guardian angels. They didn't have anything better to do, she said. What else would they be doing around here? And when we're finally safe and this is all over, the angels will float back up to the other angels and congratulate themselves for having been so useful.

I was grateful to her, but I struggled to imagine the old grouch from next door as my guardian angel. His hair was always shaggy, like a hay stack. The same colour as Grandma's oldest goat, a murky brown. But in contrast to the goat, he wasn't friendly at all. Watched me and Rami over the fence, as if we'd shake his apples from the tree as soon as his back was turned. Those apples were his pride and joy. Large, shiny, red apples.

OK, I admit it, I did pick the odd one. But not very often, I promise. He always had some complaint or other to discuss with me, or Mum, or Grandma. It was only my father with whom he had no problems. He'd often sit on the veranda in the evening and play chess. His wife was very shy, always scurrying around, her head bowed. Was one of those women you don't notice, even when they're there, and when they're not there, even less.

'Someone like that can't protect me,' I said to Grandma. 'How's that meant to work? She's so feeble.'

So Grandma brought over a soft silk scarf, held it directly under my nose and said, 'Well then, blow her out, right now. We only need the angels who are going to help you.' That sounded so crazy I had to smile.

A few evenings later, I found a fragrant red apple on a white porcelain plate on my bedside table. I thought of the neighbour and decided not to eat it, even though I knew the fruit's white flesh would taste sweet on my tongue. I just inhaled and enjoyed its unmistakable scent. As the room grew dark, Grandma came over to my bed. Sat down, lit a beeswax candle. The light flickered on the ceiling, our huge shadow heads bobbing above the window frame. She wrapped her loving arms around me. I put my hand on hers, felt the protruding veins under my fingertips. I could barely see her face but I knew she was smiling.

'Tired?' she asked.

'No,' I said.

'But of course you're tired.'

We fell silent and listened to our breathing.

'The apple's from the neighbour,' she said. 'He wants you to know, you should try it.'

'You bought it at the market,' I said.

'It was the last one on the apple tree over there,' she whispered. 'It was waiting for you. Hanging there all this time, just for you. Try it and think about something good. Then everyone will be happy.'

I snuggled up and tried to believe her. It was pointless asking any more questions. Maybe it was, maybe it wasn't. I would never know.

No. Of course I haven't forgotten my cat. Just as Rami hasn't forgotten his friends. I'll go to him and tell him to blow out his memories, just like Grandma did with me. Instead of the scarf, I'll just have to use toilet paper, but that'll be fine. I reckon loo roll will work.

Laura has a friend from nursery called Lynne. I really like her. Sadly, she doesn't go to our school. It's such a shame because if she did, we could go around school as a three. And that would be really, really fun. Her parents own a plot of land down by the lake. It's quite far away, that's why she's not here. Such a pity. I don't see her very often, but when we're together, it always feels so normal. Completely normal. So weird.

Our German teacher, Mrs King, the one who's taken a liking to me, is our form teacher as well. That means she's responsible for us and everything to do with us. She's usually sorting stuff out for me because nothing is ever straight forward. *You're a work in progress*, she said once and laughed, so I knew it was a joke. I was pleased we were standing in the hallway and it was the end of breaktime. The pupils came along jostling and shouting as normal just before the bell rings. Someone rushing past, suddenly remembering something they have to do. I smiled too so she knew I hadn't taken it the wrong way. She often sits with me in one of the classrooms after school and goes over the work I didn't understand. She gives me extra exercises and brings me books. If I don't understand quickly enough, she gets impatient. As if I don't appreciate her help. As if my gratitude and the speed I learn go hand in hand.

I don't want to disappoint her. I do try. Even Laura's mum praises me when I do my homework with Laura. Laura's not as good in German as most of the other girls, mixes up the letters, but only when she writes. I always do that. Always make loads of mistakes. Even Laura does better than me when we get our homework back. Her text is usually sprinkled with red, but mine's a red sea. She scoffs at our rivers of blood; she thinks it's hilarious. I'm not so keen on this joke. Laura's really good at speaking. Witty. Doesn't miss a beat. I don't just fall flat on my face, sometimes it's my whole head. When I'm meant to speak, I hesitate, and the words clump together in my mouth, like bricks. Feels like I'm choking on them, on everything that's tumbling around in my brain, and if someone laughs, it gets even worse. But I know I just have to go for it, all in one go, otherwise I won't get through it and the laughter will grow, as more people join in.

'Copy me,' says Laura. And she smiles her rebellious smile. Lopsided, just raising one corner of her mouth.

Looks natural on her face, with her strawberry blonde fringe on top. 'Open your mouth. Like this.'

And then she starts to show me how.

'Stop it,' I say, 'I'm not your dentist.'

But that doesn't stop her.

'I had to practise at first, too. You can't just do it.'

I can't ever imagine Laura being shy. She probably came into this world with that cheeky, lopsided grin on her face.

'You know they used to take the piss out of me?' she says.

'No.'

I can imagine that even less, Laura having the piss taken out of her. Cool Laura in her jeans with the strategically placed holes, on her thigh, for instance, but not too high. With her checked boots and flowery shirt with a skull on it.

'All the time. I felt like a tiny little mouse.' Laura gestures, holding out her thumb and forefinger to show me just how small.

'Why?' I ask. What was it that made Laura a target for such meanness, like I seem to be, attracting it like some godawful magnet?

Laura hesitates, studying her boots. 'When my parents were divorcing, everyone kept gossiping about us. It was horrible.'

She suddenly stops talking and I know she's hiding

something. I know her face too well, when she glances away. So she doesn't have to look me square in the face and have her eyes betray her. But I won't insist. I hate it when someone wants to know more than I want to tell. 'Where are you from? Why are you here? Is your country poor? Is that why you're here? Do you have electricity where you're from?' And all the other idiotic questions that only idiots ask, because a halfway decent person would never ask anything so stupid.

I prefer to leave her in peace. I'm surprised. Other people have secrets too, sealed off by fear. I'm not alone. It sounds really bad, but I'm kind of pleased. Because Laura's secret brings her closer to me. I hug her, at first she pulls away, then stays still, we stand chest to chest, until I start to feel her nipples begin to harden. Two small sharp points under her skull shirt. And it makes me flush badly, bright red, all the way up my face. I start sweating.

Our teacher, Mrs King, asked me if I want to go to her place to practise. That's so bizarre; she doesn't do that for anyone! But the school year is nearly over and she's not very happy with me because she wants me to pass. She clearly wants me to. She could just wash her hands of me. There are others who are also in danger of failing, yet she doesn't invite them. Always makes such a concerned face when it's about me. Like she's got toothache. No, as if I had toothache and she's got to share the pain, and she's a bit annoyed that she's got to feel it too.

Ha! I'm the best in the class at rope climbing. None of them could do it as fast as me. Am so proud. Not everyone can do that.

Went to Laura's after school.

'Hi, Mum,' Laura yelled into the house.

No answer. Strange. The radio was on in the kitchen.

We went in and saw her there on a chair, a half-filled glass in her hand. An empty wine bottle on the kitchen table in front of her. Glassy eyes and flushed cheeks. Just sitting there. Watching the pasta bake burn.

Laura turned off the oven and took out the charred pasta bake. 'I'll set the table,' she said in a cheery voice, as if everything was completely normal. It sounded rehearsed.

'I'll put out the glasses,' I said.

Today was so awful. Had a speaking test Laura had forgotten all about. She's convinced she's messed it up completely. I was called in an hour later and was so nervous I could only jabber complete drivel. Such a crap day. Laura decided we should console ourselves so invited me to McDonald's after school. I'd never been there before.

Always driven past it on the school bus and seen the brightly coloured price boards displaying the different meal deals. Rami kicks up a fuss if we're so much as nearby, almost pulled Mum's arm off once. Wanted a hamburger. The toy too. Some colourful plastic tat. Obviously, he's never had one. And now I was there. Without him. Felt a bit bad for him, but not for long. Kind of proud because I belong now.

Stood behind Laura and acted like I'd been there loads of times before. Nothing special. And then it was my turn and it took me ages to decide what I actually wanted. Not like Laura who always orders Chicken McNuggets. Behind me, people began to murmur. 'Get on with it, young lady,' said a man in a lumberjack shirt. I was so overwhelmed I simply pointed to something. Chicken pieces with a really sweet sauce. Bit stodgy. But I still wasn't full afterwards. Not sure I actually liked it. But at the same time, I could've happily eaten a second helping. Laura laughed. She likes that. Stuffing herself silly and still wanting more.

Ate at Laura's this evening. Her brother was there too. Sat opposite me. Sort of felt like he was watching me. Didn't dare look up. Something's changed. Not sure what. And then when I did look up, our eyes met. We grinned, embarrassed. And then looked away again.

Later, Laura's mum was going to take me home and as I was saying goodbye to Laura, he came down the stairs again.

'Let me know if you ever need a hand with German,' he said. 'Laura's no help whatsoever, she can't even do it herself.'

'You're such an arse!' Laura shouted. I had to laugh.

Laura's mum steered me towards the door. 'Peace, people. Peace, love and pancakes. Now, out.' As if we were puppies.

School's been so stressy this last week. One test after another. Even worse: presentations. If Laura hadn't have given me one of her old presentations, I'd have been completely screwed. Thank God our geography teacher didn't notice. He's such a birdbrain, he doesn't even notice when he's told pretty much the same thing word for word. I hope I pulled it off. I really tried.

And then at the weekend I visited a lake with Laura and her mum. Her brother stayed at home. Apparently, he wanted to play handball. He plays in a team, a proper one. In any case, I don't think he wanted to come. Even if he didn't have training.

The lake is on a plot of land belonging to some of Laura's mum's friends, Lynne's parents. Laura doesn't see her that often. They weren't there though, had gone to

Turkey, so there was plenty of space for us. It was really pretty there.

One thing I was embarrassed about though, Laura's mum went swimming naked. Completely starkers. My eyes were popping out of my head. Didn't want to stare. But of course, I did. She's got beautiful round breasts and a plump little belly with lots of scars across it. She laughed.

'Come on, it's just us. I promise I won't peek!' she said.

Laura stepped out of her knickers and kicked them up into the air with her left foot.

I couldn't help staring at her bum, wishing the ground would just swallow me up on behalf of all of us. My mother would never do that. Neither would I. Never! It's so weird. When I think about it though, I actually have no idea how I look naked now. I don't know what I look like. That sounds ridiculous. I get changed in the toilets, so do my mum and my aunt. Or after a shower in the bathroom. There's no large mirror in there, only a small one over the basin. I know my breasts have grown; they jiggle around when I walk, and when I run for the bus, it really hurts. I've not seen them uncovered from the front. For two years. And what I haven't seen myself, I won't be showing to others. So I said I wasn't feeling great. Headache and all that. Told them to go ahead and swim without me. Still enjoyed sitting by the water.

1

Laura's planning a birthday party. I absolutely have to be there. There's still a few weeks to go but she's already pestering her mum.

'It'll be huge,' she says. 'It'll be wild,' she says. 'And it'll be late.'

And then I know that for me, it won't be wild or late. Probably not huge either. Dad's literally so strict about all that. Hopelessly strict. It'd be easier to have a party here at ours. He'd allow that. Partying under his watchful gaze. That'd be fine. I'm just not allowed to go out. None of us are. Not that my parents want to. Sometimes I think, Look around you. Nothing's going to happen here. Sometimes I think he's exaggerating. We've come through so much that was actually dangerous. A party like this isn't dangerous. Surely he can see that. But then sometimes I'm frightened here, too. At night. In the wood. Even at school.

I passed my German assignment! All by myself!

'Almost a three,' said Mrs King with the hint of a smile, like a statue of the Madonna.

I danced down the aisle to collect my exercise book. Because the tension when she walks in with the pile of books is unbearable. The silence that instantly falls over the class. A silence where you can hear every little fart, even the quiet ones. Not a deathly silence. When you're dead, you don't fart. And then she builds the tension even more by reading extra slowly. First the good grades, from the ones at the top to the fives at the bottom. And if your name hasn't been called in the threes, you start to sweat when she gets to the fours. And so often I've been one of those whose name hasn't been called. So worried my tummy aches and my feet feel like lead.

And when you collect your trophy and it's not one of the last to be called, you feel as light as a balloon. It's one of those ones with a shiny surface that reflects the light so beautifully. Dad was incredibly proud. Mum too. I know that's exactly what they're hoping for. I won't disappoint them.

By the way, Laura also nearly got a three. 'Not a five, anyway,' she said. 'Time to celebrate.'

We went to McDonald's again. This time I knew which burger I wanted. And a coke. Markus came with his friends, too. Laura was put out because she wanted me all to herself. Most of the time, she wants me to herself when someone else wants to be with me.

70

'Nice plait,' one of them said to me, and tried to touch it. But Markus said, 'Leave it.'

I ran off to the toilet and waited a few minutes until my stupid red face had cooled down.

Laura's mum, however, was really annoyed because we'd eaten at McDonald's. When Laura got to school – late, as she often is – and flopped into her chair next to me, completely out of breath, she told me she'd had an argument with her mum late last night. She thinks McDonald's uses excessive amounts of flavour enhancers and that it's extremely unhealthy to eat there. Laura called her a spoilsport. Her brother made a joke about deep fried mice in the burgers – some real meat at least. Laura lost it; she hates it when he makes fun of her. I wish my family would get upset about such trivial things.

Laura's going to be fifteen. Her mum says the good times start now. I wonder what she means by good; I've been fifteen for six months and nothing's changed. Nothing at all. Only a couple of zits. But not too bad. Mum says they'll calm down. When I'm a bride, they'll calm down. And every single time, I get embarrassed. Just that word.

I'm fed up with the skirts I wear. I want trousers with rips in the knee like Laura's. Laura's got another tear right under her bum with a seam along it. Her mum made a big fuss about the second tear that Laura had spent so much time making, and sewed it up. It's fine for her daughter to show her knee. But she doesn't need to wave her 'arse' around in front of her school friends. Not her daughter. End of.

Laura's going to see her grandma today and hasn't got any time for me. I think about mine and miss her dreadfully. Sometimes this longing comes at me like a huge wave and knocks me over. Sometimes it laps against me in the shallows. If Grandma were to sit next to me now, I'd listen to her. Tell her everything. She knows so little about school here, or Laura. So little about everyday life, about the new things, new habits, everything growing within me day by day. I do write to her, but writing's not the same. Maybe she doesn't recognise me any more. Maybe I'm already a little bit foreign. Reality is fragile. You think you're far from war and it doesn't concern you any more. But that's not true. Other people are still back home and you can either forget them and relax or think about them and worry.

I prefer to just go swimming alone with Laura. In the lake in the woods, for instance. Or at Lynne's. But I dread school swimming lessons. Every time. When we go swimming here in the small village pool, I'm constantly tugging on my dodgy old swimsuit and making sure no one notices. I spend the whole time hoping nobody spots how embarrassed I am about it.

Laura's noticed. She must have done because her mum's invited me to go shopping with them because Laura apparently needs a new swimsuit.

That's nonsense. Laura's only recently been saying in the changing rooms how much she loves her new swimsuit. A black and blue one with sporty stripes down the sides that make her look all athletic. Even Laura looks like a professional swimmer in it. So why would she need a new one? I know why.

And while we were in the sports shop, they both persuaded me to try on a red and black swimming costume and then Laura's mum wouldn't take no to buying it for me. I said it was embarrassing. But at the same time, I know Laura's mum can afford something like that. And she loves shopping. Sometimes the unopened shopping bags lie around their house for a week.

It made Laura's mum so happy. Gushed the whole time about how great we'd both look in the summer in our matching swimsuits (as if I could ever go to a public swimming pool without a teacher). I said I still needed a bit longer. Closed the curtains and just stood there. Looked at my thighs that have rounded into a curve. Not like

Mum's. More like my aunt's. My boobs. They were right. The swimsuit looked good on me.

'What's up?' bellowed Laura outside. 'I'm waiting out here.'

'Leave her alone,' Laura's mum said. 'Give her some time.'

And I held the curtains tightly together so nobody could come in. Stripped off the swimsuit. My heart was beating so loudly I feared they would hear it outside. And then I looked at myself in the mirror. And stared at my reflection. And stared. Tried to remember how I looked before. As a child. I looked so different. And a bit hairier. Like an adult. The dark pubic hair a shadow between my legs. Still don't know if I like it. Probably not. Couldn't stop staring at this strange Madina in the mirror. She looked surreal, like a picture. Wondered where the old me has gone. The one with the skinny legs and the bloated belly.

I've not told anyone at home about the gift, no one needs to know. Stuffed the bag right at the back of the chest of drawers in our room. Perhaps I'll get it out in the summer, maybe.

It's Laura's birthday soon. I'd like to give her a present. For once, give her something in return for all the things she's given me. And keeps giving. She's definitely having

74

a party. And I'm definitely invited. Like all her other girlfriends. Everyone will give her something. And I have nothing. It's me again who never has anything for anyone.

Said that to Dad today. Shouted at him to give me some money. To buy a little something at least. He went through all his pockets. Nothing but fluff fell out. I can't even buy a flower for one euro and thirty cents. I know I've hurt him.

Mum said, 'Draw her something beautiful. We can make a card for her.'

What with? The old corn from the kitchen? Screw that. And screw the emergency solution, too. I don't want to be like that any more. Ran outside and stomped around the house until my anger subsided. When I'm fuming about our few square metres, it quickly blows up into a big argument. Our small space isn't big enough for two angry people. Let alone three. Mum can try and walk the tightrope all she likes between me, my aunt and my dad. It doesn't work. I'm now sitting behind the house on the bench Dad always sits on when he's cross. He's right. It's a bit damp but the view's nice. And the birds sing. I'll go over into the empty field and pick a massive bunch of flowers for Laura. Wildflowers may not be anything special, but they are pretty.

Actually, something pretty is always something special.

While I'm worrying about presents, Laura can't wait for her birthday. As if on that day everything will be suddenly different. Magic.

After school today we sat for ages at the bus stop in the rain and let one bus after the other drive past. And Laura talked and talked: what she wants, what the cake's going to look like, how she wants to receive her presents at exactly twelve o'clock midnight . . . She'll be staying up until midnight anyway. She wants some really expensive jeans. Sexy dark blue ones. Ones where she has to breathe in to do them up. And some stilettos. Silver stilettos.

'Can you even walk in them?' I asked.

And she laughs. 'If I don't ever get any, I'll never learn,' she said.

Actually sounded quite convincing. And she wants to go out in town. With her big brother. Her mum has been promising since she was twelve. And she's been waiting, year after year. To go out. You're allowed when you're fifteen.

I don't even want to imagine what would happen if I went home in stilettos. Mum's never worn them because my father doesn't think it's right. Not for decent women. And when he speaks about decent women, he gazes lovingly at Mum. And then he shoots a look at my aunt, as though he's sure she'd go out wearing stilettos all the time, even into the mountains given half a chance. And my aunt usually holds his gaze, narrows her eyes and then looks like a cat that's about to pounce.

The bus driver looked at me and Laura sitting in the bus shelter in the pouring rain – shoes soaking, wet hair plastered to our faces – and stopped. Rivers of water under the tyres, a waterlogged road. Brown water in brown mud. And we waved him happily on: *No, we're staying here.* The driver looked at us as if we were crazy, and drove on. As did the next one. And the one after that. Until the cold seeped into our clothes.

I don't like PE. No, I hate PE, more like. The PE teacher herds us together like goats and we scurry around the hall. To 'warm up'. To warm up, I put woolly socks on! And a scarf! And then, when we're 'warmed up' – or sweaty – the real torture begins. Using our combined strength, we have to build barricades using a wooden box with leather on top called a horse, and then we have to jump over the horse. Goats jumping over horses. Just as weird as it sounds. I do PE barefoot because I don't have any trainers that I can only wear in the sports hall. In the school lost property box there aren't any. And the tracksuit I had at the beginning was too big for me. The trousers once fell down to my knees and everyone could see my knickers. And they weren't particularly pretty either. And then there's always this feeling of never being enough.

Even though I'm quick. And can easily do somersaults. It doesn't matter because, despite having a body that is fast and flexible, it's still out of place. Because it looks different and smells different. I wear embarrassing, borrowed clothes. And they don't. And it's really hard to grasp that. I will never be like them. Even if I had the best outfit, my own beautiful room and went to the hairdresser every day. My fears would still be there. The way I flinch when someone nearby moves too quickly. I just have to get used to it: not being like the others with all their wonderful things. And their confident laughter. But I'm still great at climbing ropes.

Laura's taken pity on me. Again. Brought me a small bag. With a deodorant in it. And some make-up. Feel really, really uncomfortable. I'm not a beggar. I know she means well and I'm ashamed it irritates me. I know I need what she's giving me. But I still don't want to be on the receiving end. Again. Always.

'Don't beat yourself up,' Laura said. She knows me very well now. It's not just me that knows what she's thinking just by looking at her face. She does it to me, too.

'My mum doesn't use the eye shadow any more. There's not much in it. And besides, it's not for you, it's for your mum.'

'Oh right,' I said, and then felt miffed that the pressed, pale grey-green powder case wasn't for me. The colour wouldn't have suited me anyway. Nor Mum either. But she loves doing herself up. I know she'll take the powder that looked so pretty on Laura's mum's eyelids – with her light skin and grey eyes – and put it on her dark skin and it'll look fake, artificial, weird. Like she's pretending to be someone from here. I catch myself thinking how I hate Mum for it, briefly. But my skin is no different to hers. Our foreign skin betrays us. Sometimes I just want to peel it off. Like our whole backstory. Sometimes I wish I'd been born here, knowing nothing else but Laura, Sabina and the teacher. And Laura's brother too. Know as much as they know. Or as little.

What I wrote yesterday was unfair. I know. But strangely, I'm not sorry.

Sometimes I wonder why I've been so unbelievably angry recently. But sometimes I really welcome it. This rage brings me to life. Then I can feel. When I'm sad, I barely feel anything. Almost nothing.

Don't beat yourself up.

8

When do you begin to question everything? It's started happening slowly. To me. Thoughts pop into my head that wouldn't have crossed my mind before. And at the beginning, I was ashamed of it. But less and less so now. Because ... because our lives are changing, for God's sake. And we were happy when they began to change. Because everything that changed saved us. How happy we all were. To have crossed the border. The threshold of the police station where we were held that first day. The gateway to the reception centre after that. The first meal. The first doctor's visit. Arriving here at our boarding house. School. The first German words. We were all so happy. Overjoyed. I wanted to know everything about life here, try everything. And the more I tried, the more it changed. And suddenly it was going too fast for Mum and Dad. Then they put the brakes on.

From the first words came many. From the first trips to the authorities came several. From the joy of the new came fear of the future, for Dad and for Mum. But not for me. It feels like this here is the future. In this language.

In this home. In this place. I know I have a future here. I don't want to jeopardise that. But I question other things. Dad's detachment. Mum's silence. My aunt's maliciousness. And why Rami is literally always, *always* put first. In everything we do, he is treated better. And there's only one reason for that: he's a boy and I'm not.

That seems so unfair now. He's younger than I am. The family pet.

Laura's just picked me up. You can't imagine how pleased I am. Peace and quiet at last. And space. Perhaps Markus will be there after all. Laura said he's out with friends. Maybe sleeping elsewhere. I'd be disappointed, but relieved.

Time passes far too quickly when I'm there. It's evening already. And I've got to stand up from the comfy sofa and go home. Quiet music and the TV playing in the background. I'm stuffed and feeling sleepy, the cake in my belly pressing me down further into the sofa, as if it weighed a tonne. Laura's already put on her pyjamas and bed socks, everything's all nice and cosy around her and I stick out like a sore thumb. I say I don't want to get up. Don't want to leave either. Actually, I'd quite like to sleep here.

'Call your parents,' suggests Laura. 'Can't imagine it's a problem. Not for us.'

And I grin and stand up because while it's certainly not a problem for her, for me it most certainly is, a big one. Dad would never allow it. Never. I don't even want to ask. No point. He'll never behave like everyone here. Makes me sick.

So I stand up.

And Laura's mum says, 'I'm going out this evening. Stay until I'm ready. I'll drop you home in an hour.'

And I call my father using her mobile, which he could never contact me on in an emergency because he's got no credit on his phonecard. And have to beg for this one extra hour. Tell him nobody's missing me at home. And I suck up to him, and he gives way because I promise to do everything I can possibly think of, and I hate myself for it.

I observe how Laura's mum gets ready to go out. While Laura and I were watching TV, she ran a bath. Positioned candles around the edge of the tub. Red, scented. Sprinkled a handful of rose petals into the water. With a dreamy smile. Like she was performing a magical ritual. Sat on the edge of the bath staring into the water, the flames reflecting off the surface, and lazily trailed her fingers through the petals. As if caressing the water. She was wearing a pale green towelling bathrobe. In the humidity of the small bathroom, her hair curled even tighter than usual and her cheeks were flushed, her whole face glowed. I'd so love Mum to do something like this, just once, enjoy a quiet moment, just for herself. Then I'd be even happier. Then I'd know I don't have to look after her. Because she can look after herself.

What I've just written is ridiculous. How is she meant to do that in our scruffy shower cubicle? When there's always someone outside, waiting to get in. Where at best she might have a bar of soap, at worst, nothing but towels that are as rough as newspaper – how can she ever relax like that? That's what Dad's for, to be there for Mum. Laura's mum doesn't have that. She bathes alone, dances alone, sings alone, goes to sleep alone. And perhaps she's not happy like that either. Last time I was there, Laura sneaked the empty wine bottles out of the way.

There were loads.

'We had some friends over,' she'd said quickly.

I nodded. I know nobody else has been round except for us. For a long time. I've also noticed that Laura's mum has a wineglass in her hand the whole time we're there. And it never stays empty for long.

Mum would be miserable as sin without Dad. And with Dad there, she worries about everyone else. Just not about herself.

I love lazy Sundays so much. I mean, those Sundays that are actually lazy. There's not many of them. That feeling of slowly waking up, no alarm piercing through to tear you from your dream world. Rolling over again and going back to sleep. Knowing you can. Nobody's waiting for you. Nobody wants anything from you. Nobody's making demands or expecting anything of you. Being a good daughter, a good sister, a good friend, a good pupil. Just a normal girl. On Sundays like this, peace reigns. When it all comes together.

By Sunday afternoon, all that peaceful Sunday quiet has sometimes flown out the window. For instance, if Rami goes upstairs to see the weirdo, because despite the fact the weirdo hurts Rami, Rami's literally obsessed with the scumbag, because he's older and stronger and all that. And then he comes back down, he starts telling us everything he's heard upstairs. Things like, we ought to fight for an independent state.

And my father frowns and asks, 'Which state?'

And Rami beams and says, 'A state. Our own state.'

And Dad asks him whether he knows what a state is.

Rami shakes his head. And then he says, 'And in this state, only true beliefs are allowed. All the others are bad.'

And Dad instantly begins to rage and relaxation is over. And Rami howls and hides under the table because he now doesn't know who's right or why everyone's angry. I can't properly explain it to him. That topic gives me the creeps.

Today I went running. First time. Didn't dare go far from the house. Ran backwards and forwards until the landlady asked, 'Is everything all right?' Even spoke pleasantly. Can't imagine she'd be worried about a problem with the pavement; it's not her street. Or perhaps she was worried about it. But either way, I was involved.

'Yes,' I called back to her, turning around again, already somewhat breathless. 'Yes, all OK, all OK.'

She shook her curly head and then withdrew it back in through the window like a tortoise, the whole house her shell. Pulled the white net curtain closed behind her.

Laura once showed me a video at hers, an old one, she said. She'd enjoyed watching it as a child. A giant tortoise crawled into view. It had a really weird name. I can't remember its name and now I can't stop thinking about that silly old tortoise, like there's nothing more important going on in the world other than its silly old name. Feels good.

I run back and forth again. And as I trot towards the woods and the balls of my feet start to hurt, I just keep thinking about the tortoise's name. It looked like a mountain, a muddy brown tortoise shell mountain. With trees on top. And yes, surrounded by swamps. Deadly swamps that make you heavier and sadder. That's it, the hero's horse died in there, but not him. Because he had to live. Who else would've saved the world?

It was *The NeverEnding Story*. It started off as a book that Laura loved. It was made into a film as well and of course, she had that too. Unfortunately, I didn't fully understand the book. The film was much easier. Laura told me she watched the film over and over when her parents were getting divorced. Before that, she'd spent hours reading the book. She laughs about it now, but she's embarrassed about it, a bit embarrassed anyway. Back then she wanted to *be* in the book. Disappear into it. Into that world. Where wishes are fulfilled. Difficult to do it permanently. Didn't manage it either. Even when she put her whole face into the book and closed it firmly around her head. On the pages with her favourite pictures, the ink's run a bit because she'd once cried over it. I saw the marks. The paper's warped. Very slightly like waves over the surface. You can run your fingers over them. Even with your eyes closed, you can still find the spot.

She moved on to watching the film, over and over, especially when her parents were fighting. When you're just reading, you can still hear everything. But when you're watching a film, you can turn it up really loud and when they come to complain about the volume, they stop shouting at each other. For a while anyway.

I don't have anything at home I can turn up loud

when Dad has a go at my aunt. He doesn't shout at Mum as often.

I stand still for a moment, bend over, looking down at my trainers, catch my breath. I'm pleased my feet hurt. Means I can feel them again.

She was ancient. And her name was Morla. If you let it go for long enough, everything you think you've forgotten comes flooding back. You just have to let it go. Ancient Morla. In the Swamps of Sadness. She didn't care about anything. And you had to outwit her.

That's what I'm going to do now too.

I pant the whole way back along the stretch. Can't run any more. Stitch, like someone's stabbing me with a knife. I'm not in as good a shape as Laura, who regularly goes running. She's copied that from her mum, who used to go running with her husband. When they come back from their runs, they have red cheeks and a look of pride on their faces, they even smell the same if you get close. Almost like sisters. I want to feel pride like that. But this stretch was too short for that.

Tomorrow we're going to Lynne's. So happy. What a *pity* Rami's staying at home. Mum wants to do something with him.

It's warm today. Even into the early evening. We're sitting in Lynne's family's garden. Laura's mum, the other guests and Lynne's parents are drinking wine on the terrace of the old farmhouse. The plot is huge. Age-old fruit trees and flower bushes and plenty of wild grass. They don't 'look after' their garden like Laura's mum does.

'Nature needs freedom,' says Lynne's mum, Manuela.

I'm not so sure about that. If you let nature do what it wants, we'd have lice and worms and other illnesses. And you'd stink.

I don't dare say out loud what I'm thinking, though. There are loads of people here. Old and young. Everyone chatting and eating. The table's made from a giant piece of wood, sanded and oiled, resting on two lumps of marble. Some sort of natural oil. It smells. On the table there are candles, their flames fluttering in the breeze. An aroma of grilled fish stuffed with mint and lemon. Lynne's dad has cooked for us. Manuela hates cooking, can't cook either. Good that there's someone who can do it for her. I don't know any men, other than him, who like to cook instead of their wives. It's funny. Now she's taking care of the guests' drinks. Helps him to carry the plates to the kitchen. A beautiful lantern swings in the breeze, its cut-out pattern casting splashes of light onto the table and people's faces. Above the lantern, on the barn wall, there's a swallow's nest. Every so often, birds shoot past performing breakneck manoeuvres, diving in from up high, down into the mud nest and whizzing quickly out again. Swallows are amazing. I recognise them from back home. I'd watch them for hours, lying on my back in the garden. Back then.

We've stuffed ourselves so much we can hardly move. The idea of swimming hasn't even been mentioned. We're lying on an enormous rug – it must be four metres wide – next to the lake, gazing into the water. Between us, there's a china plate with lemon cake on it that tastes almost like the one my grandma used to make. Somehow when I'm at Lynne's, I'm reminded a lot of home. I can't work out why.

Lynne was the first person who reminded me of home. While she's completely different to me, she's not as different as Laura. Lynne has dark hazelnut brown hair and eyes. Her skin is almost as dark as mine.

Laura pokes at her slice of cake until there's a square smiley laughing back at us from the plate.

I dip my hand in the water. It's warm. Small fish swim around, come closer. I break small pieces off the deconstructed cake and drop them in the water. They pounce on it; for a moment, the water looks like it's boiling. They're not very big, just so many them.

Lynne holds onto one of her legs and pulls it up so her foot is almost behind her ear. Not showing off. Just because.

'Amazing,' says Laura, without a hint of jealousy.

Laura's not very sporty. She's not that bothered about her jogging, let alone gymnastics. Lynne's mum was a professional dancer before she got married. Lynne showed us some photos and videos today. Of her mum.

'Is she a ballerina?' I asked. Somewhat disappointed. Because she wasn't wearing one of those beautiful tutus where the women look like elves. Otherworldly.

'Nope.' Lynne shrugged. 'But whatever. Manuela's cool, even without a tutu.' She doesn't call her mother 'Mum' or 'Mummy'. She uses her first name. Sometimes when she's joking around, she'll even just use her surname. Ms Rolf. 'It's called performing,' she explained to me. Manuela performed. There are videos. I've seen two of them. I liked one of them. I just didn't get the other one. She just moved really oddly, waltzing across the floor. 'Good' wasn't quite the word. Absurd, more like. But very agile. She moved as a scorpion carries its sting, her feet up above and behind her head. And Lynne used to do it with her. Stretching exercises. Dance classes too, when she was little. And now she goes to dance workshops. But she's not sure whether she wants to dance. Sometimes she prefers theatre. Whatever it is, she wants to be on a stage. Any stage. That much she does know.

'When the curtain goes up,' says Lynne, 'a whole new world emerges. Every time. Sometimes it's beautiful and sometimes it's ugly, sometimes it just doesn't go well . . .'

She eats another piece of cake and licks her lips. 'But hey-ho, it's not the be-all and end-all.'

Her father works in theatre. 'Can I go and watch sometime?' I ask.

'Difficult,' she answers. 'Can you speak Turkish? Exactly. You won't understand. Most of his shows are in Turkey.' That's where he's from. But he's lived here for ages. With Lynne's mum. And Lynne reels off a list. He's done films. Plays. Radio programmes.

'Do you often go?' I ask.

'Occasionally,' says Lynne. She makes it sound so obvious. She travels to Turkey and comes back again. By plane or car. Easy peasy.

I feel horribly jealous. It fills me so quickly, like a blocked toilet fills with brown water when you try and press the flush. It soon begins to trickle out my ears.

He's not from here, just like my dad, but it's all so different for Lynne. He can speak for himself. Lynne doesn't need to interpret. Lynne never needs to explain anything to him. He knows the score. He speaks German, albeit with a strong accent. Sometimes I don't understand him at all. But still miles better than my dad.

I look over at the adults on the terrace: Lynne's dad is waving his arms around. He's clearly 'performing' with glasses and plates, playing them with forks. He even manages to get a rousing melody out of them. Everyone laughs. He beams. My dad hasn't beamed for ages. I know that's not good. He'll be sad for ever.

'Does he work here as well?' I ask.

'Yep, more and more,' Lynne replies. Last year, here at home. He held a small week-long festival. People came and slept over. But it was the holidays, so it was fine.

'How can you act if nobody understands you?' I ask again.

'You can still perform,' Lynne gestures. 'Of course you can still act. Actually, you can do anything. You don't need to be perfect.' And she belches.

Oh my God! And she's not even bothered! It'd be nice to be able to let myself go like her sometimes ...

'Heeeey!' says Laura. She doesn't like it when I'm impressed by someone else.

'Didn't pay its rent, had to leave,' Lynne laughed.

'Next you'll be farting,' says Laura, somewhat irritably.

'Shall I?' asks Lynne, lifting her bum into the air.

'Don't you dare!'

Her mum comes over, wearing colourful, wide-leg silk trousers, the fabric's so similar to the cloth my grandma's clothes were made from – roses, colourful patterns. And on her top half, she's wearing nothing but a white bikini top, her beautiful tanned skin and giant ivory earrings that swing in time as she moves her head. She holds her head very straight, her throat stretched out. Dark hair streaked with grey, piled high on top. Undyed. But very elegant. She's in such great shape you can see each individual muscle around her belly button. Like she's never had a child. In the background, Lynne's father roars and Laura's mum laughs.

'I have to go home,' I say regretfully.

It'll be dark soon.

9

Been to Mrs King's every afternoon this week. She's got a small flat in the next town along. Not far from school, unlike me. A small flat in a shared block with a little garden in front. The garden's bordered by huge conifers so that nobody can see in. Means it's always in the shade. Two shiny colourful china balls on posts stick out from one of the flower beds. And an iron raven next to the front door. So real ones don't come near.

On her desk there's a photo of a man in a beautifully mottled, dark wood frame. He's wearing glasses and has a moustache, one of those properly old-fashioned moustaches with curly ends, like the kings in fairy tales. All he's missing is a goatee on his chin. The table's crammed full. She has to push some piles of papers to one side to make space to sit with me. Exercise books. Newspapers. Handwritten memos. I tried to help, but accidentally caught the wooden frame. The moustached man tottered and nearly fell over the edge. She grabbed it with both hands, just in time, but in doing so knocked a pile that started to lean and slide, a white paper avalanche spilling across the desk and the floor. Essays, tests, notes.

'Don't touch them!' she shouted at me, her voice completely different to normal.

I pulled back in fright.

The weirdo upstairs has suddenly decided he loves me. Keeps hanging around the hallway. But what a coincidence, only ever near our door. After dinner, he waits unusually long in the dining room, even after he's finished and his family have already gone back to their room. Looks a bit odd. I like this even less than the pestering from before.

Rami can't get enough of him. I refuse to go and fetch Rami from upstairs when he's been up there longer than he's meant to be. Mum has to go now.

After having avoided him for a week, he actually spoke to me.

'I've got something for you.'

'What?'

'A new idea. A future.'

'Thanks, I've already got one.'

'That's what you think. They treat us like filth here.'

It's true. But only sometimes. And not all of them.

'Think about it,' he says. 'Come on up and I'll tell you more.'

I have a bad feeling about this little chat. Smells a

bit fishy. I've developed my own inbuilt radar. When you've been caught in the middle so many times before, you hone it. Like a warning light that flicks on when someone comes across all friendly but still seems peculiar. Makes you think, 'Watch out!' At home, I swiftly had to weigh up what I could say to whom. I had some friends who I suddenly couldn't see any more. Our parents forbade it. One girl who I'd been to nursery with slammed the door in my face when I went over to study with her. And through the door she'd said, 'Get lost. My family wants nothing to do with traitors.'

'You're crazy!' I'd said.

Back then, I didn't really understand what was going on. Why that kept happening. I still hadn't seen our cellar. That was just the beginning. She never answered the door again. Only her mother appeared at the window, waving her arms like you do when you're shooing chickens out the way. Or stray cats. Then she swooshed the curtains closed. That was my last conversation with her. A week later her house was flattened. The family moved out. To the city, apparently. They never came back.

There were some neighbours I used to drink tea with in the afternoons. They didn't even say hello any more. At the beginning it was confusing. But then people started to disappear. And you got used to being careful. And then you got used to the silence. Rami struggled, though. Mum was more talkative. Smiled more. Told cheery fairy tales.

Took homemade bread to the neighbours. Even when she wanted nothing more to do with them. She bakes really well. It smells so good barely anyone can refuse. And the smile, always that beaming smile. Mum's secret arsenal. Unfortunately, Rami really enjoyed going on these missions because he always hoped he'd be given a sweetie. Almost turned Mum's secret weapons into an own goal.

When you visited, you had to be on your guard constantly to make sure Rami didn't let anything slip. Rami was never allowed in the cellar. But sometimes he heard things. Noises. Screams. And then he started asking questions. And when he got no reply, he'd take it further, going to the neighbours, to the people on the streets, even. Asking what he could hear in our cellar. Whether they could hear it too. And then Mum would smile a particularly broad smile and mention his blossoming imagination. And I told him there was an angry monster living down there that only Dad could feed, so it wouldn't eat us. He turned pale and started bawling.

And I impressed upon him, 'Yes, yes, you can cry. But don't you go downstairs or *crunch!* You'll be gone. And don't tell anyone. The monster doesn't like that. It might just creep up the stairs.'

Rami pondered. And then a shadow fell across his face. 'But where will we go when the bombs start falling again?' he asked shakily.

Yes, that was a tough one. 'To the neighbours',' I replied.

'And if they're not there?'

I sighed. 'Then to the monster. It wants to survive too. When there's bombs, it won't do anything to us.' I would never have believed such nonsense.

Mrs King serves me tea. As a reward and a break before we carry on. Tea with milk and sugar. A hint of spice, although I'm not sure which. A pleasant taste though. Two biscuits come with the tea, oblong, something dry. I thank her graciously. I always make an effort to be particularly polite and helpful around her. It's all a bit embarrassing and pretty strained. But I am grateful to her; I need her. Don't have a choice. No choice at all. There's a crucifix hanging above us, a dying Jesus stares directly into my teacup.

She stirs her tea with a silver spoon and a look on her face that suddenly grows calmer the longer she stirs. Almost smiles. Drinks tiny sips. Peers into the tea as if into a cauldron. Savours her biscuits. I watch her, spellbound, so much so I stop paying attention to my own hands and teacup. Tea spills over and I hurry to fasten my lips to the edge of the china. Choke and cough brown drops onto the polished wood of the table and the exercise book in front of me. Close my eyes and before she starts shouting, I wish I could simply disappear into thin air.

'Teacher's pet,' someone hisses at me in the corridor. 'Arse-licker.'

I walk quicker. He laughs. Someone else joins in. You're not allowed to cry, otherwise they call you a cry baby as well. Having a go back isn't a good idea, either. Just makes them get louder. I drop my head forward, down into my shoulders like a tortoise, and just walk on. But not too quickly. And not too slowly. Like nothing's happening. Like with dogs that growl as you walk past.

I sense a large group has formed behind me. You can feel something like that. The hairs on your neck prick up like antennae. Anyone who's ever lived like that for long enough develops a radar system to be well warned in advance. Ridiculous really because it doesn't usually help. At home, there were rockets smashing down all over the place. Where the soldiers wanted them as well as where they didn't, more luck than judgement, not like the targeted bomb attacks. You knew where they'd planted the bombs. You knew who was wearing the explosives jacket and where he was before he pressed the button.

We didn't have any anti-aircraft systems like that. I'd heard how the men sat in the sun on the benches in the market place discussing it. Who had them and who didn't.

Naming countries I'd never heard of, naming other men I don't remember. Dad never wanted to talk with them. He sat away from them and kept quiet but they turned on him, first questioningly, then mistrustfully and finally angrily.

Having a system like that would have been great. Definitely.

I'd like one too. Before they can open their mouths and send the next stupidity flying towards my back. Or over my head, pulled in tortoise-style. And then I think how luxurious my problems are. Words aren't bombs.

I always try to get to the car park as quickly as possible, preferably unnoticed. Once I'm there, I clamber into Mrs King's car. And return to her table, paper towers and tea.

Today, though, the name-calling idiots run after me. I pretend to be concentrating hard, looking out of the corridor window.

The sun's been shining all day. I'd much prefer to be walking through the woods to the lake. Dangling my legs off the bridge. Gazing into the dark green water. Up to the sky.

Watching the butterflies in the bushes, but catching none. The bumblebees buzzing.

No senseless chatter.

I slam the door in the idiots' faces. Outside it's stiflingly hot. Muggy. Over on the mountain tops, dark clouds gather.

'Do you carry her bag for her?' they call. 'Do you clean her toilet?'

I wish a storm could be unleashed right now, striking the whole group with a bolt of lightning.

'You're doing well,' says Mrs King and smiles. Pleased with herself and me. 'We'll get there.'

I nod respectfully. She nudges the biscuits towards me. I take one, even though the dry crumbs get caught in my throat, I can't stand these oblong clumps of sawdust any more.

'That's real shortbread,' she says. Sounds like she's saying, *That's real gold.*

'Thanks,' I say, chasing it down with tea that tastes as good as always.

She waits for me to say something else. I chew silently. She scratches. She's feeling talkative. She'd really like a chat. But I'm too tired to help her. And have no idea how to begin. She runs her fingers along the varnished surface of the table.

'Don't you want to know what it is?'

I nod. *Yes.*

'It's a traditional Scottish biscuit. Very fine.'

Pause. You can hear my teeth grinding the traditional Scottish biscuit.

'I brought them back from the UK. As a souvenir.'

'Nice,' I say, because I can't think of anything better than that. I just want to get away from the stuffy room and go home.

'I often used to visit the UK,' she says. 'I lived there. For a few years.'

She gathers the cups, places them on the small tray where the shortbread's sitting on a blue patterned china side plate, and clears it all away.

I stare after her, her very thin back enveloped in a tight-fitting, dark red and green tartan dress, tights in summer, flat shoes with silver sparkles. I stand up.

'I'll tell you more tomorrow,' she calls from the kitchen.

10

Laura says goodbye to me like I'm off on a global expedition. Sabina's poorly and she's got nobody to gossip with. I don't think she's got it that bad. I'd love to not have anyone to gossip with and just head for home. Instead, Mrs King's already hovering by the exit, a long dark shadow in brown shoes. She's holding her car keys and a file. Inside it, my collected sufferings. On the way there, she tells me she spent a long time living in the UK. In a country house. I imagine this house covered in tartan like the clothes she wears: the curtains, the upholstery, the carpets, the wallpaper. Everything in black and red tartan. She was happy there.

The weirdo's there again. Presses a flyer into my hand.

'Read it,' he says conspiratorially. 'Then you'll understand.'

I glance at it: young men in war gear. Wearing headbands with writing on them, standing on tanks, flags fluttering in the background. I don't need anything that looks like the past. I give him back the paper. 'That's not for me,' I say.

Laura's going swimming with Lynne. I've got to go to Mrs King's. Ouch!

I hate Rami so much. The little rat! As always, he's painted me out to be the angry one while he's the angel. Every single time we fall out in front of Mum and Dad. He's the most manipulative person I know. Madness.

The last few days, I've started taking some bread back to our room with us so I can feed the birds in the tree outside the window. Turns out Rami saw me and dobbed me in to the cook. And for his honesty, she gave him a reward. And of course, I got told off, first by her, then by Dad, who has absolutely no feelings for animals, and finally by Mum, too, because I'd had a go at Rami.

On the side table there's a candle burning. Next to the candle there's a photo. I catch sight of it as I walk past. Too small to make out anything from afar. The framed photo of the man with the moustache has a bunch of flowers next to it. Mrs King's in a strange mood today. Doesn't shout. Seems absent. Doesn't tell me off much. Silently reads my word creations. As we sit here drinking tea as always, I notice her eyes filling with tears.

'Is today a special day?' I ask. Sounds wrong to call it special, although they do have days here where you're meant to sad. Good Friday, for example. Or memorial days. Minutes of silence. I used to miss the fact these days were special a lot of the time and sometimes got it wrong; not happy enough, or sad enough, or serious enough. Didn't know enough to play along.

Mrs King nods. Briefly wipes her eyes then quickly puts her glasses on. Only then does she look at me. Through her glasses, her eyes look different, smaller, further away, I can't see the tears any more. 'He died ten years ago today.' She stands up and walks over to the table. 'My William.'

I follow her. In the second photo, she's standing next to her husband. She's hugging him. She looks younger. And she's laughing. She has wonky teeth and her hair's sticking out. She looks a bit like a horse, but a very happy one. He's chubby, dressed in a suit and tie. A tartan tie. He'd started curling his moustache by then, but it's not as long as on the other photo. He had a small bald patch, too; he already looked quite old.

'That was just after our wedding,' says Mrs King. 'We travelled to London afterwards.'

I nod.

'My English wasn't exactly brilliant,' she continues.

105

'I found it really hard to abandon my German, but I wanted to be with him.'

I nod again.

'Be a love and fetch the teapot from the kitchen,' she says, sitting down.

The kitchen's very narrow, a thin tunnel between two dark brown veneered rows of cupboards. It smells of beeswax candles. Tins of tea all over the place. Piles of them on the shelves. Many of them are empty. She collects them. I find the teapot, a quilted cat tea cosy on top to keep it warm. I pull the cat off the pot like taking a hat off a small child. Pick up the teapot. Dad drinks tea too when he remembers. Not so easy to give up your habits when you're older. Interested to see if I pick up anything like that. Drinking coke, perhaps. With Laura.

When I come back with the tea, she's sitting down, slumped in her flowery armchair, the biscuit tray on her lap. I feel a bit sorry for her. But then, she feels sorry for me, too.

'I was so pleased when his aunt took pity on me and began practising with me,' says Mrs King. We both sigh. 'Milk?'

I nod.

Lynne sends a message via Laura saying I shouldn't be so hard on Rami. She can talk! She's got a cool mum, a zany dad, a large house all to herself and a party basement. And no siblings. I'll happily lend him out. Then she can see what it's like.

It's such a nightmare when you have to be grateful to someone who properly gets on your nerves. I can't stand Mrs King any more. But I'll be here at least three times next week. Before the last assignment and again before my speaking test. I have to pass this test. I have to move up a year. I can't lose Laura. That's why I sit here with Mrs King, hour after hour, staring at her cuckoo clock, waiting for the bird to pop out of its little house, chirping for a few moments of freedom before being swallowed again by the hole with the loud ticking mechanism. Her words ring in my ears. She wants me to put everything in its place and create an internal display, like a butterfly collection: take the words apart, analyse them, order them and place the meaning of every little thing in a glass cabinet with all the right letters the right way round. So many words, so many meanings, so many rules. Snares hidden in the long, complicated sentences that I fall into, landing splat on my face.

Laura's annoyed because I don't have any time for her any more.

Fat lot of good I can do about the fact Mrs King keeps abducting me to cuckoo clock land! I'm only doing all this so I can stay with Laura. Is she really that thick she can't see it? Like I enjoy it!

Of course I'd prefer to spend time with her. Leave school together as usual. Walk along Landstrasse, past her house to the square by the church. There's a café opposite. Incredible cakes just waiting under a glass counter; I can even see them from the bus stop. Apple cake. Chocolate cake. Nutty swirls drizzled with icing. My mouth waters just looking at them. Laura goes there sometimes when her mum's not home and she doesn't want to be alone and can't be bothered to cook. Her mum complains because it's a shame to throw away her pocket money there when her fridge is always full to bursting. There's so much in it, she regularly has to throw away mouldy food. I'd love to go there with her. Sometime. And now she's meeting Lynne and Sabina there instead of me. Great.

Laura and I fell out today. About maths. Doesn't actually happen that often, but every so often it does, when we're both stuck on an exercise and Laura's mum can't help us. But today it was somehow worse. Think I annoyed Laura.

So then I went home without having done the maths homework and copied it from Sabina the next day. Had to promise to put her chair up on the table for her at the end of class for a week, so the cleaning lady can clean under it. I'd never make demands like that.

Told Mrs King at breaktime I wasn't feeling well. That I might throw up at any minute. I rubbed my belly and retched a bit until I actually brought up some air.

Mrs King pursed her lips. She took a precautionary couple of steps back and then sent me to the school nurse.

I have to lie here on the leather examination couch for the whole hour until the lesson's over and we're officially let out. I'm staring at the patchwork blanket on top of me. It's made up of brightly coloured little squares. Each one made by a different pupil: trees, flowers, animals. The lower school ones are all a bit scruffy and uneven. I run my fingers along the stitched-on rows of pearls, bored. Imagining creeping out of the house in the middle of the night. Moonlight on the trees. Eagle owls, like the ones drawn here, peering out of the holes in the trees, the bark a dark purple and velvety blue against the night sky. A red strip of light where the sun has gone down. The first pale stars. I tiptoe out of the house, my aunt's moonstone gaze on my back, I see her hunched-up figure in the window, high above, her dark silhouette against the room's soft half-light, and I know the others are all fast asleep. They sleep, Mum's arms around Dad and Rami snuggling in between. Dad snores loudly, Rami quietly. And my aunt with her bitter stare watches over this night as the one before and the one to come. Sometimes I think the moon wouldn't come out without her night watch, no twinkling stars. Amina, the silent queen of the night. She stands there and watches after me but she wakes no one, doesn't call out, lets me go. The grass is damp, the moss muffles my steps, no one hears me, no one sees me as I set foot into the woods. I disappear noiselessly between the tree trunks. Animals call in the thicket.

The breaktime bell interrupts my daydream and the night-time wood crumbles. The tangle of voices in the hallway swells. A knock at the door, impatient, keeps on knocking because the school nurse doesn't call 'Come in!' straight away, then the door flies open, bashing against the wall that's clearly been bashed before.

The school nurse frowns. 'Please don't do that again.'

And Laura storms in, throws her arms around me and says, 'I'm sorry.'

For us, the journey home is a friendship ritual. Laura hates it when we have to go home separately. As always, we wait at the bus stop. Sit next to each other. Laura waves at me and walks home. I travel onwards. Alone. Without her, without the troublesome Rami. Gaze at the landscape and watch people getting on and off. There's something calming about this ritual. My little bit of me-time, ring-fenced for me alone, the warmth of spending time with Laura carrying over. And then I'm happy to see Mum and Dad. Tell them about my day. Mum always wants to know, every day. She wants to know what I've been doing outside. Whether I'm all right out there. Through me, she tries to understand what I'm learning. To figure out this country. Perhaps to stay close to me. Think that's important to her. More important than to Dad anyway. He wants to figure it out but doesn't want to listen – bad combo, very bad.

Sometimes I want to shoot Mrs King rather than be grateful to her.

I've been a real pig. Ungrateful, loud and mean. Sometimes I'm ashamed of myself.

Final exams in six weeks. I think I'll pass. This hellish cuckoo clock land will not have been in vain. I've promised myself that. And Laura. And my parents. In that order.

I'm caught in the tea trap. Mrs King screams in endless loops and bangs the German book down so hard on the desk that our teacups rattle. I close my eyes tightly. And I'm there again: bare feet on soft moss, giant bark-covered tree trunks. Animals in the darkness. A coo. A screech. Something with leathery wings swoops over my head.

111

I duck. Not everything that comes from above is good. From pigeons, for example. Wonder if griffins poo in dollops or pellets. I'm back in my fairy tale wood.

After school, some older kids are standing by the gates smoking, hanging around for one of my classmates. I'm waiting for Laura who had to run back for the loo, despite having been twice already.

I stand there and suddenly realise that one of them's staring at me. Very odd. Not unfriendly. They come over and ask if I want one. I hate cigarettes. I connect the reeking odour with Dad when I used to help him in the cellar. When someone had died, he'd smoke one after the other as he bandaged the injured and administered medicine. And those in pain always wanted to smoke. The haze that hung between the cellar ceiling and the mattresses. It was often stuffy down there but with this smoke cloud, it was unbearable. I don't get why you'd do it voluntarily. Those stinking fingers that would hold onto me as I tried to leave. 'Stay. Stay. I need water.'

I hate the smell. I hate it. Smells are intertwined with memories, ten times more than anything else. The worst thing is the smells, then the images, then the sounds. I still can't bear it when some fool or other lets off a flare. I could throw up right there and then, wet myself from fear. The memories suddenly appear as if turned on by a switch. Zero to a hundred. I'm pleased Dad doesn't smoke any more. It means Daddy-smell is free from those memories.

Laura eventually arrives, grabs my arm and pulls me away. 'We don't smoke,' she says. She doesn't smoke. But Markus does. Half in secret. Enough that you can still find the butts near the house. Chews gum after every smoke so Laura's mum can't smell it.

11

It's Laura's birthday party this weekend. Hope Dad doesn't fly off the handle. I have to go. Everyone who's important to Laura will be there.

Haven't dared to ask Dad again. He's still annoyed with me. Because I so want to go. He just doesn't get it. Despite all the niceness.

'We're starting at eight,' says Laura, pressing an invite into my hand. 'But you're coming early to help me.'

'Of course,' I say. That's the least of my problems. For Dad, daytime is harmless. Like dangerous things only happen at night. I think that's a blatant misjudgement. You can get off with someone anytime, any place. Sometimes in the school playground I don't know where to look for all the couples everywhere, pupils twisted into astonishingly brazen, smooching pretzels. And sometimes they even kiss each other with their eyes open! They peek mid-snog, looking past their kissing partner to see if anyone's noticed. And when their wandering gaze catches my eye, it's so embarrassing I don't know who I'm more embarrassed for, them or me. Others parade love bites like some kind of trophy. At home there were war medals, for injuries, outstanding achievements and particularly selfless acts. And here they have medals for love.

I'm pleased Laura's not like that, for now. Sometimes she fancies some boy or other, but never enough for me to be worried. I wouldn't like her to be going around arm in arm with someone else, somebody else allowed to snuggle up to her. And I can't even begin to imagine being part of one of those pashing pretzels myself. Dad really has nothing to fear. But if he is concerned, he should really think it through properly. I mean, several of my classmates have already had sex at school. A couple in the ceiling space and another pair in a toilet cubicle. I heard the ones in the loo. Wanted to get out of there quickly, but then stood at the wash basin and listened to the muffled sighs. The sound of damp skin on damp skin. It was disgusting and exciting at the same time. I was all over the place after that.

Rami's properly in trouble. It's only fair. He should get it sometimes, not just me. He knows what makes Dad angry. He knows him. But no, he had to go and borrow a plastic gun off the weirdo from the second floor and come crashing down the stairs, fling open the door and scream 'Batatatatataaaa!', pointing the gun at everyone and pretending to shoot us all with a machine gun. He'd not put a bullet through half of us before Dad got to him, tore the gun out of his hand, threw it on the floor and jumped on it.

Rami's mouth dropped open and stayed that way. Then he let rip. 'But you've broken it, what am I going to tell him upstairs?'

And Dad roared like a bull. Each roar embellished with a jump on the weapon. 'When' – *crack!* – 'will you' – *crack!* – 'finally learn' – the plastic completely fell apart and Dad stood there breathing heavily, collected up the bits and lay them neatly on the table – 'that violence is not a game?'

'What am I meant to do now?' spluttered Rami.

My mother stood there gaping. To be honest, so did I a bit. Where would we get the money to pay for it, I wondered, but better to say nothing.

'War is not funny,' yelled Dad one last time, so loudly his voice cracked. 'Weapons are not for fun! Weapons kill, you idiot!'

And Rami wailed, 'He'll kill me! He'll kill me!'

And Dad grinned and said, 'Just let him try. He'll soon see.' And he rubbed his chest and added quietly: 'War breaks people. In this place, everyone should know that.'

Later on, I see Mum meekly begging Mrs Boss for a Sunday job to earn a little money, at least.

Two days to go and I still don't know what's happening with Laura's birthday party. I got a three in maths. Cool or what? That's softened Dad up a bit. But he says he still needs to think about it. What else is there to think about? Wouldn't he want to go to *his* best friend's birthday party?

Well. There's so much to tell but I'm really not in the mood right now. It'll take pages. No. Can't be bothered.

Rami's obviously realised I'm writing everything down. He's always hanging around my bed where I keep my diary under my pillow. If he even *thinks* about it ... I always close the little lock before I leave the room. And take the diary with me to school in the morning.

The weirdo from the second floor is waiting for me again outside the dining room after dinner. Or for Rami. Who knows? Leaning against the wall, all laid-back. Looks odd. Rami goes to run over to him, I pinch his arm and hand him over to Mum who hasn't noticed anything. They leave. As I go to follow, he blocks my way.

'Why are you against the one good idea we've got going on here?' he barks at me. 'Join us.'

'Don't know what you mean,' I say.

I try to keep walking. He grabs my arm.

'Of course you do.'

'Leave me alone.'

'You'll see who's right,' he calls after me. 'And you can tell your father that too.'

'Tell him yourself,' I hiss.

'Yes, that makes more sense,' he yells. 'Who wants to talk to women about things like that? You've got no idea.'

'Piss off!' I shout and run up the stairs.

He chases me and catches me by the hair. I duck out the way and move quicker. He's left holding a single strand. I slam the door behind me and lean my whole body against it.

Dad looks up from his book. 'What's wrong?' he asks.

'Never let Rami up to the second floor again,' I say, panting for breath.

A forbidding look comes over Dad's face again and he steps outside. The hallway is, of course, empty.

Caught Rami red-handed trying to open my diary. Pulled his hair. He didn't even try to play me off against Mum. Mum doesn't put up with him trying to nick my stuff.

I'm so angry! So angry I don't even want to write.

Hit myself with my pillow while everyone else was already at dinner. No way I'm going down there.

So, Laura's birthday party, the big event – which I can only go to with my *stupid little brother*.

The plan was that I go home with her after school and help her and her mum to get everything ready. And Dad's great idea: after that, I just leave. If I like my friend that much, I can cook with her and then come home. Dad's version of a party. I banged my school shoes on the wall. And yelled. He didn't.

'That's how it is,' he said. 'Get used to it.'

He stood up silently and left the room. Mum followed him.

'I hate you,' I bellowed once the door had closed. 'Let's go back! Just leave! I want to get away from here!'

My aunt walked over to me, smiled at me. I'm never sure whether it's an evil smile or a genuine one. 'Be careful,' she said. 'Be careful what you wish for. Sometimes it ends badly.'

I sat down on my bed with my back to her and stared at the wall. She carried on speaking, undeterred.

'Don't do it. You'll regret it later. You only have one father.'

I remained quiet and thought to myself, I only have one best friend and I'll lose her if he keeps messing it all up.

'I know how it feels,' Amina continued. 'My father banned us from lots of things too. But I found a way around it. Without arguing with him. And when he died, I was so pleased we hadn't fallen out. There are ways.'

'He wants me to be here,' I said. 'He wants us to really arrive, properly. Doesn't he? Doesn't he?'

'To arrive, first you have to truly leave.'

'But we fled. How are you meant to truly do that?' I retorted. 'Mum didn't even have time to pack. We hardly took anything with us. You know that.'

'We've all had to pay for what he was doing.' Amina was almost whispering. 'And my husband and I the most . . .'

'What do you mean?' I probed. That . . . That is very curious.

But Amina withdrew back into her hunched position, a look of astonishment on her face, as if she was surprised she'd said all that.

'Has it got something to do with your dead husband?' I dug further.

'With my murdered husband,' she said, emphasising the *murdered*. 'Enough now.'

Amina made out as if Dad had killed her husband single-handedly. My father would never do something like that. My father's a lifesaver.

I've tried three times now to write down the story of Laura's birthday party. And I've still not managed it. I get so angry I could grab my diary and hurl it against the wall. And Rami with it. He's frightened of my outbursts now. Not that it helps. He needs to watch his back, I have to tolerate him and we've both had it up to here. And Mum's snappier than ever because she sees how much it's getting to us but she can't change any of it because Dad's gone from stubborn to super stubborn and barricaded himself behind, 'We've got to act all traditional now, so nobody ever forgets who we are.'

Dad banned me from celebrating with Laura. Seven o'clock on the dot, I was meant to be home. Very funny. The party doesn't even start till, like, eight!

We argued like crazy. Amina mentioned something he's to blame for. No idea what. And my parents have never said anything about that. Perhaps she's finally lost it. Not that improbable. She's definitely insane and comes out with something new every day. Delightful. I don't know whether to question her again. It's, like, so *confusing*, constantly finding these shards of an adult mirror, trying to piece them back together again correctly. A fragment of information from Dad, a splinter or two from Mum and another slice from Amina. I can't complete the puzzle by myself. Really, I can't. By the way, Laura keeps telling me I shouldn't say 'like' quite so often. It's, like, so annoying.

Whatever. I went crying to Laura at school and told her everything. She was really pissed off too. She doesn't want to celebrate without me. She asked her mum to help. In some ways, I'm really pleased I'm so important to her.

That evening, Laura's mum called the hostel. She worked her magic on Dad. Mrs Boss stood next to us and listened to me interpreting. Stood there, like, blatantly *watching* me, as if Dad and I were this evening's TV programme. Disgraceful. I turned my back on her and carried on talking. I'd have loved to fart and then innocently ask her if she'd let one go. But I wouldn't have dared.

Laura's mum put on her responsible voice. Promised to drive me home. Suggested he should think about Laura too. Word of honour, she'll drive me home. At ten.

I know the party's going on till midnight. But it's better than a kick in the teeth.

I haggled all-out with Laura's mum, like I was at the bazaar and either didn't have enough money or only had lousy goods to offer. Dad was really only an afterthought.

Laura's mum proposed he come and pick me up. Then

she could show him the garden. He could do some gardening for her, if he fancies.

Dad's rationale was under attack. I know how much he wants a job. And money. He's fighting himself, what he wants against how he thinks he ought to suddenly behave. And then all at once, he agreed. I rejoiced. And then he went on, 'But Rami has to go too. No Rami, no party.' And he'll collect me. In person. At ten.

I forced myself not to lose it. I was almost tempted to simply misinterpret it. To say, I can come on my own.

I could lock Rami in the wardrobe in the hallway that afternoon. He fits. He often hides in there. But I'd have to gag him too. I couldn't do that. I couldn't stand to do that any more, use force to hold someone's mouth shut. I don't ever want to have to do that again in my whole life. I had to go along with their plan voluntarily. It was as good as it would get. I could see that.

Laura's mum suggested Rami would get bored. With the big kids.

'That's fine,' said my father.

And Laura's mum said, 'Great. Then I'll pick Rami up in the afternoon, when the girls get here.'

Right at the end, my father repeated he'd come over.

In a voice she uses when she rolls her eyes, finding something tiresome, Laura's mum told him he was most welcome. The earlier the better, so it's still light. Then he could have a good look at the garden.

The carrot in front of his donkey nose that gives me a little bit of freedom.

Dad had a serious chat with the weirdo's father. They walked round and round the yard, worried looks on their faces. The weirdo stood watching out the corridor window upstairs. When he saw me with Rami in the yard, he shook his fist at us.

Another day over. I'm tired. Nothing's fun at the moment. I'm worried about the summer holidays. I'll be stuck here the whole time. Horrendous. Not even the cat shows her face.

Sitting in Mrs King's living room. We've just come to the end of the language torture. The end of my wits, too. For all Mrs King's good intentions with these extra classes, it seems she wants to put the cherry on the cake today, her crowning glory.

'So?' she asks me, as I start to pack up. 'Do you know yet what you want to be?'

Nothing immediately springs to mind. I think about it while I'm stowing my books in my rucksack. I've never actually thought about it. Always just as far as the next test. To the end of the next half term. And the furthest I've ever looked ahead is as far as school report day.

'I don't know,' I say uncertainly. 'A doctor perhaps?' Yes. That feels good. Something I already know. That I know will be needed.

Mrs King frowns doubtfully and says, 'No, that's not for you. That's too ... complicated. What about receptionist?'

The weirdo from the second floor has disappeared. His parents are beside themselves and the police have already been. Dad says he's just probably run away and he'll come back when he gets cold and hungry. It's quieter without him.

Having an internal battle. Want to ask Dad about Amina. Not sure I can. Don't know how he'll react. I'm frightened.

Can't hold it in after all, so I ask Mum. Mum turns pale. I don't let it go. What's wrong with Amina? She ought to trust me. I'm a big girl now.

'Amina's always been strong-willed,' says Mum.
'So?'

That's hardly an explanation.

Mum stammers. 'Amina didn't behave as she should.'

'I don't always either.'

Mum looks at me in shock. 'Madina! That's not funny!'

'Dad says she's a fallen woman,' chimes in Rami, who's wandered in. 'Do you think she hurt herself?'

'Oh shut up, Rami. Go away,' I say. 'Get lost!'

He whinges but still goes.

I got a bit out of Mum. Not a lot.

Amina should have married a man my grandfather had chosen for her. But Amina clearly didn't want to. And picked her own husband, dead Uncle Amir.

I don't think it's all that bad. What's all the fuss about?

Went straight home instead of going to Laura's after school. Lost so much time for nothing. Laura's mum picked us up later on. Flew up to the house with the top down on the car and her hair still in curlers. She wore a colourful scarf over the curlers so no one could see them. Dad stood in the doorway to greet her. And to start with, he was quite taken with her outfit, from a distance. Seemed relieved. Until he saw the curlers. Then he frowned.

When he comes halfway to his senses, he's usually sorry for raging and yelling. But he can't ever apologise.

He's not one to back-pedal. Then he looks all remorseful yet annoyed at the same time, and he just ignores whatever happened before.

Laura's mum climbed out the car and shook Dad's hand. Mum just stood there and smiled and smiled. Everyone meeting for the first time. Laura's mum dragged the huge plastic sack from the car. The clothes she'd gathered for us. The neighbours looked on enviously. Mrs Boss seemed rather nervous. I don't think she wants other people to see inside her boarding house. We stood there, Mum and Dad on one side, Laura's mum on the other. And in the middle, me and the plastic sack. Me caught between everyone again.

It was weird. Like one of my worlds suddenly colliding with the other.

I hope Laura's mum wasn't horrified. By our house. By the rundown yard. She didn't say anything. Mum thanked her. Had picked a bunch of flowers for Laura. The second bunch from us. Oh well. Dad picked up the plastic sack. I sat down on the back seat. Rami clambered in next to me. I kicked his shin. Rami didn't dare say anything. Laura's mum put her foot down. 'It'll all be fine,' she said and winked at me in the rear-view mirror.

Rami got out of the car looking scared. I think it was the first time he'd been so far away from our parents all on his own. I almost felt sorry for him.

Laura came flying out of the house. Threw her arms

around me. You could smell her a mile away! A cross between candy canes and car air freshener. Her first perfume. I wondered whether she'd chosen it herself or if she'd fallen victim to her grandma. Was wearing her new jeans. And her silver stilettos. For once she was taller than me.

She looked down at me and said, 'You can barely see your parting from up here, you've got so many curls. Amazing!'

'Take your shoes off,' called Laura's mum from the house. 'You'll trip over in the garden.'

'Whatever,' Laura replied, not complying, despite the huge blisters that had taken just an hour to start growing. Every third step, her heels would sink into the grass and she had to keep stopping to yank them out. She looked a bit like a stork in fancy dress. Red lipstick. She never usually wears red lipstick. Looks unfamiliar on her face. Too grown-up. I don't like them.

We prepared the table, hung the lanterns in the garden, strung a colourful sign saying *HAPPY BIRTHDAY* above the terrace doors. Brought out the cake, the pizzas and the salad. Lit the barbecue. The special smell of food wafting from the fire. Vegetables, cheese and meat. Almost like us when we used to celebrate. A lazy summer's evening, the grill sizzling and the beautiful full moon above the treetops. Stars as delicate as embroidery starting to appear faintly against the darkening sky.

On the one hand I'm feeling happy, on the other, sad. *Here* can't simply replace *there*. The present can't replace the past. Simple as that. The present can only lessen the past, disguise it, cover it over. Then you don't feel it as deeply or as piercingly. But it's still there. And when Laura and our school friends look up into the rose-tinged sky and laugh, they know only this sky, only these clouds, only these chirping birds that we're keeping awake with our racket while all they want to do is lie down and sleep. But I know other stars, other animals, other smells and they're never far away. And when I see Laura being hugged by her grandma, it makes me melancholy because I miss *my* grandma so very much. And then I feel sorry too, because I don't want to disturb Laura's party with my sadness. So I smile and smile. Even as Laura's grandma leaves and sneaks Laura another envelope with a conspiratorial look. Laura doesn't like her grandma much. I've often told her she ought to be happy because she has a grandma. Honestly.

I reach for the teardrop I wear around my neck. Caress the stone that's grown warm from my skin and promise myself that I will see Grandma again. I'll wait for that moment. And then I shake my head, shake away the thoughts, take a slice of pizza and swallow the feeling that comes with the first bite.

Laura's in a birthday frenzy. She's speaking really quickly with a high, almost squeaky voice. After an hour she's already croaky. She laughs. She's really and truly happy and wound up to two hundred per cent.

Rami sits in the living room in front of the huge TV and finally, *finally* gets to play assassins. In virtual reality. With Markus. Rami's even happier than Laura; I'd put him at three hundred per cent. He's concentrating so hard on the controls he doesn't make a sound. His knuckles have turned bright white. His face is blotchy. Wouldn't surprise me if he gets sick from sheer ecstasy. He's completely forgotten his job to watch out for me. He is Altair and he's on an important mission.

Laura races between the laden birthday table and the front door. The doorbell rings every five minutes. And I run around after Laura like a little dog. For one thing, her enthusiasm's infected me and I'm so excited I can't bear to sit down, but also because Laura needs me; without me she'd keep toppling over.

The garden fills up. Laura's mum pops a cork. There's fizz. I get the impression she drinks most of it herself. The long-stemmed glass firmly in her hand.

She's wearing a dress that glitters so gold it's like a pearly liquid, a backless, sequined dress. She's also excited and very, very proud. I take photos of Laura and her mum. In front of the apple tree that was planted when Laura came into the world. In its branches hang colourful fairy lights and two large illuminated plastic flamingos. Laura's face in the pink reflection glows feverish.

She hugs me so tightly I can hardly breathe. In part because of her perfume. 'Fifteen years ago today, right here,' she whispers in my ear. 'Dad planted it here. It's as old as me.'

'That's good,' I say. 'Be happy you don't have two flamingos hanging from you. They look much better on the tree.'

Laura's dad isn't here. As always. I've never met him. Laura doesn't speak much about him. All I know is she meets him every couple of months. Briefly.

Laura's drunk a whole glass of fizz. I'm on guard and don't drink anything. It's nine o'clock and Dad will appear soon. I hope and pray that Laura's mum won't be completely plastered by then.

Markus comes and tells me Rami's fallen asleep on the sofa. His pleas to share Markus's energy drinks went unanswered. Pleased about that. I'd have been really angry with Markus.

Markus says, 'I'll check whether my old games console in the loft still works. Then you'll get some more peace and quiet.' And he gives me a quick hug.

Above us, lanterns made of rice paper. Colourful chinks of light on our skin. I feel a bit giddy, despite not having drunk anything. I could stay here for ever. It'd be beautiful. Even if Rami has to be here too. We could just all live here together. The house is huge, there'd be enough space for everyone. Markus' arm lingers around my

131

shoulders a second longer. I brush his fingers. On his wrist, he wears a chunky silver watch that reminds me of a prison ball and chain that he's dragging mistakenly around his wrist rather than his ankle. Maybe it's an astronaut's watch. With that you must be able to float through the cosmos and still know what time it is. I look at the dial: it's half past nine. My carriage will soon change back into a pumpkin, I'll flee and lose a glass trainer. And somewhere deep inside burns a tiny glimmer of hope that Markus might just look for me.

I go to the garden fence. See Dad's silhouette approaching in the dusky light. He walks swiftly. Marching like he marched as he led us through the mountains and away from our home. Alert and ready for battle.

Then he stops and stands. We look at each other over the fence. I open the garden gate for him. Dad steps into the garden. Tense and serious, wearing his best shirt, his trousers ironed. His trousers look properly old-fashioned. Haven't seen him wearing ironed trousers for ages. It's hard to get an iron from Mrs Boss. It will have cost Mum some favour or other that she'll have to fulfil. I silently promise to help her with it. Whatever it is. They've both done this just for me. It's very sweet of them.

Dad's very nervous, follows Laura's mum, who goes to offer him alcohol and then at the last moment remembers what I warned her, so offers him juice instead, and steers him through the party guests. He hates juice but is too polite to refuse, so he takes a glass and sips from it. I follow behind and take the glass at the earliest opportunity. She makes a broad gesture that's meant to describe the whole garden and asks if he can mow lawns. And trim bushes.

'Yes,' I say, without waiting for his answer. 'Yes, he can. We had a big garden.'

12

'Well that turned out all right,' Laura says on Monday. 'Actually went quite well. He didn't kick off. Mum now has a gardener, your dad has a job and we have peace. A classic win-win-win situation . . . God, I feel awful. I think I'm going to be sick.'

Laura's impressively green in the face. A sweet pistachio green. On Sunday, she'd been drinking again with her mum, grandma and family friends.

'Can we go to the toilets. Now.' She burps. It doesn't smell good. 'Your father clearly learns quickly. Unlike mine.'

'Why, what's up with your dad?' I ask directly for the first time.

She throws me a look, quite a gloomy one, but that could just be down to all the partying and nothing else. 'Oh, leave my dad out of it,' she says. 'I'll tell you about him some other time.'

She looks absolutely shattered. Bags under her eyes, hair a mess. She's really not well. Every breaktime I go with her to the toilets. 'I think I'm gonna throw up,' says Laura over and over, without ever actually doing it.

I stand next to her in the narrow cubicle and place my arm around her shoulders while she kneels before the bowl. On the wall next to us, there are various messages. *Here in the toilet lives a ghost who haunts . . . who stays too . . .* Some of it's crossed out with felt tip. And written next to it, the letters *AUA*. At nose level I read *Love makes you sick.* Hmm, not just love.

Laura arches her back and retches. But nothing comes up other than spit. When she turns to the side to speak to me, the reflection of her half-turned face swims in the toilet water. And behind it, an alarmed half of mine. I wonder what I'll do if she collapses. The flush isn't working properly, water constantly drips. Our reflected faces in little waves.

'What are you staring into the toilet bowl for?' says Laura irritably. 'D'you think we'll find treasure at the bottom?'

She's got a red mark on her neck. I know exactly what it is but I pretend not to have seen it. That mark worries me.

'I drank everything out of order,' says Laura. 'That was stupid.'

I've no idea what she means. I nod so she sees I'm taking it seriously. She says nothing about the mark. That makes me nervous. I want to know who she was snogging on the night of her fifteenth birthday and who I need to go after.

Laura's kept looking at her phone the whole way home. She checks it every few minutes for new messages, probably from the love-biting vampire. I feel like a right gooseberry.

By the way, the weirdo from the second floor still hasn't come back. That is unusual. I didn't think people here could disappear like they did back home. I hope nothing has happened to him. The police were here again. Everyone was questioned. I said I thought he'd started saying strange things.

One of the police officers pricked up his ears. 'What exactly?' he asked, and I got scared he thought I was somehow caught up in the whole thing.

'Just nonsense,' I said evasively. 'Can't remember what exactly.'

It keeps eating away at me so I pluck up the courage to ask Amina. Because today can't go any more wrong. I ask her straight out. Stop her in the corridor and bundle her into the toilets with me. We're completely alone. She looks at me like I've just asked her if she fancies a stroll on the moon tomorrow.

'What have they told you about me?' she snorts. She bares her teeth. They're sharp and white. On the upper left, a tooth's missing. When she pulls her lips back like now, you can see it really clearly.

'Honestly speaking, absolutely nothing. That's why I'm asking.'

'Are you up to something?'

'I'm really not. I just want to know what's going on.'

'They despise me. That's what's going on.' Amina goes to leave the room. I hurry after her.

'I don't.'

'Like that helps.' And she's already swept out. I trail behind.

'You can't stop now, please. I just don't understand any of you any more. Please,' I beg.

Amina shrugs. 'It's not as straightforward as you think.'

I wonder whether that's true. Clearly there's something going on. I trot behind her and think to myself that the way Dad treats my aunt isn't right. It's the first time I've thought that. How he treats her used to seem completely normal. Because that's just how it was. And because she was unbearable. And since she's been with us, I've hardly seen her any other way. Perhaps that isn't fair.

Laura keeps messaging the new guy she's met through Markus. Every day, all the time. Fifty messages each. Her phone is always nearby. On the kitchen table while we're studying, or pretending to, at least. When we're lying on the rug in her bedroom listening to music or reading magazines. As soon as it vibrates, Laura quickly turns away and looks at the screen with an expectant smile on her face. And grins and grins. But she doesn't reply straight away. Doesn't look like she's *not* bothered about him, but then, what do I know? I don't even have a phone to message someone with. And I wouldn't know who to message either.

The door opens and Markus peers in, glances at me and tells Laura there's been a change of plan and her mum wants to eat out tonight. 'Around seven.' Pauses for a moment. 'What about you? Are you coming?'

'No,' I say.

'Shame.'

He always looks bored when he's talking. So cool. Grown-up. I notice how long his arms are. He stands in the doorway and stretches. Crazily long arms, like a monkey. And I smirk. Markus, monkey guy. He sees it, gives me a strange look – this time I can even sense a hint of uncertainty in his gaze – and disappears.

Laura's phone vibrates, she giggles and turns away. And I go back to my magazine, or at least I pretend to.

Mum asked whether I'm ashamed of our family. Well. Not of our family. But how we live here, yes. She pressed her lips together as if I was blaming her. Of course it's not her fault. But it's still uncomfortable, all crammed in. We can't afford anything and Dad's behaviour doesn't help. And I just keep getting it wrong, even when I'm trying so hard to get on board with life here. Shame is repulsive, but it's even more repulsive when you're ashamed of the shame.

Laura has no time today. Must be because of the vampire. It's the stupid lilacs guy, Christian, one of Markus's friends. The one she'd held hands with a couple of times a few weeks back. No further details. She usually tells me everything. I'm startled and a bit angry; I'm all over the place. Don't know why. Can't ever tell Mum and Dad that Laura was drinking alcohol. Otherwise I'll never be allowed to see her, that's for sure.

In history we're learning about the Second World War. The pictures come at me like echoes from my own past. They slaughtered people here, just not as recently as back home. And the teacher explains it all with such an ingratiating voice, how awful it had been. Like she'd been there. She shows photos of soldiers, prisoners, mountains of corpses and hanging bodies.

I remember how we'd leave the village to gather the bodies of the fallen that lay in the fields after a torrent of bombs. Many lay there as if sleeping, others with torn-off limbs. Others just shapeless lumps of red flesh in bits. In the middle of the field, huge craters. In the craters, body parts. Or just earth. Sometimes the soil beneath my feet was sodden with blood. Once I threw away a pair of shoes that was covered in rusty red mud. I wouldn't have put them back on for anything.

We left soon after that. That was good, as I don't think I could've gone through that any more. As we gathered the dead, we were in constant fear that the planes would return before we had finished. There were lots of us, mainly women and older people. Some were sick. Men lay on the ground before us, no women. And leaving them there wasn't an option; their bodies had to be buried so they could finally depart this world. We paid our last respects, in which we begged for peace for them. I sometimes helped. Mum often did. Amina would always go, and she'd go with a passion, as if it might bring back her dead husband. But perhaps she simply had no fear. Of being caught by the returning bombers. Or by the fighters from either side. She was far, far removed from our fear and our shaking.

And the teacher tells us how here, people were herded together like cows and killed, with calculation, order and cleanliness. Barbed wire fences, barracks, gas chambers. I can imagine all that only too well. Our war was dirtier.

More chaotic. Less efficient. But not because our war leaders were any more honourable. They'd have done exactly the same given the chance. And while I've never spoken about it out loud, I feel the need to share this with the teacher. No idea why. Perhaps because it's similar, what happened here. Because it reminds me that in some way, we all have experienced the same thing. Probably like the rest of the world. People kill. Everywhere.

I put my hand up and say, 'I've also seen how people are killed. Back home.'

A strange look comes over her, she clears her throat and says, 'I'm so sorry.'

In that instant, I'm disappointed with her. Although that's probably unfair. I can't bear to hear that phrase any more. It comes out when someone doesn't know what else to say to me and they mean it well. But it does nothing for me. Absolutely nothing. I don't want 'I'm sorry'. I just want to share what I've seen. To be allowed to say it. In front of others. And I start to speak again.

This time she cuts me off, saying, 'That's not part of what we're learning about right now.'

Mona comes over to me at breaktime and says, 'Save your horror stories.' And she blows a raspberry through her pouted lips, directly into my face. It sounds like a fart. 'You're just trying to make yourself sound important.'

I feel my hands instantly balling into fists. And my fists would just love to fly into the middle of her laughing mouth. Over and over. Until her teeth fall out. 'You have no idea about anything,' I hear myself say.

And one of the others who usually ignores me says, 'Madina's right.'

I'm surprised, and at the same time, very pleased. Just for that, I don't hit her.

The weirdo's parents have gone too. Moved out. Not deported. Now I'll never know what happened to him. But I've got a really funny feeling.

Dad's just been to Laura's mum's. Whenever he comes back, he seems a bit happier. And we've got some money. The first thing he did was buy Rami some new trainers. And a T-shirt for me. Didn't spend any of it on him or Mum. That's so kind.

Laura's mum has given Dad some jars. Filled with pâté, and pickled vegetables and jam. We haven't got a fridge so she thought about what might help. Well-considered help is the best.

I feel incredible in my new T-shirt. My own. Not

donated by anyone. I mean, it's normal for my father to buy me things, right? It's a great feeling, being normal. A little bit, anyway.

Mum's overjoyed that Dad and I are finding our way. She's so proud, like we were dealing in world politics. And as if she were the saviour of the world. She's been singing to herself; she rarely does that. She kisses Dad. Dad leans into her and closes his eyes. They sit snuggled up together on their mattress, the blanket covering their feet, and Mum sings quietly and Dad listens to her. My mum has a really beautiful voice, unlike Amina. When Mum tells us how she'd have liked to have been a singer, my aunt throws her a snide look. But says nothing, as usual. Mum sighs briefly and shakes her head, as if it'll get rid of her old dreams, like a horse shaking off flies from its mane. My grandfather forbade her from doing it and my mother obeyed. She was the good daughter.

I really feel sorry for Amina. It's not a bad thing not to marry someone you don't want to marry. Nobody here would do that. And no one would think it wrong.

Asked Mum this evening whether she has to do something in return for the iron. Of course she does. You get nothing here otherwise. Clean the stairs and mop the hallways. This weekend. I'd actually planned to see Laura, take a trip to the swimming lake. But I won't leave Mum in a bind.

'I'll help you,' I said.

She looked pleased. The buckets are heavy and there's no lift.

It's tough carrying the buckets up and down and her back aches. I can tell because she holds her back and sticks her belly out, as if she were pregnant. Rami, of course, doesn't have to help, even though he was at the party, too. When I think about that, I feel a twinge, but I force myself to swallow it down, into my belly where there's already quite a lot in storage. Running out of space in there.

We scrub the disgusting old stairs, up and down. The steps are made of wood; the wood is old, the varnish splintered. You have to be mega careful not to get any splinters under your skin – or worse, under your nails. That's where it hurts the longest. Mum's finger once got infected and swelled up to the size of an aubergine.

The kind neighbours don't walk on the stairs until they're dry; the ones that aren't put out or need to go somewhere in a hurry. The mean ones do it on purpose, so we have to clean up after them again. One older lady, who Mum always argues with about Amina, often waits for when Mum's scrubbing and then takes extra trips up and down the stairs. And Amina rarely thanks Mum for protecting or defending her. In any case, she's never helped scrub the stairs.

So today we're mopping as we go along and, of course, out comes the stupid old lady from the third floor, waits until we've done two sections and tramples down the stairs in her outdoor shoes.

On the step before us, she slips and goes sliding past, wailing, hands grasping the bannister tightly. I have to laugh. But that just makes her madder. She sits on the bottom step, groaning. But she's been brought up well and no really ugly words come out of her mouth. Nothing more than some half-hearted insults that just make the whole situation even funnier. At school, nobody would react quite like that. No, I'm really not frightened of her. Even Mum smirks to herself. I love her so much right now.

And then when we're finished, we lock the buckets, the cloths and the broom back in the storage room and give the key back to Mrs Boss and then we go for a shower. Mum lets me go first. She waits outside until I'm finished.

For a while I've been making the most of the time when I'm all alone. Behind a safely locked door. Just me. My skin, my hair. Study my reflection. My face is changing, becoming narrower, my cheekbones stick out. Laura likes my cheekbones. I'm not so used to them yet. This time I just glance briefly in the steamed-up mirror so I don't keep Mum waiting. She's standing in the corridor outside the bathroom, bath towel over her arm and toothbrush in her hand, a proper hygiene warrior complete with sword and shield. I scurry past her, slip into our room, my skin damply warm, my clean nightie on top. Such a wonderful clean feeling.

In the room a cosy half-light reigns. Rami's been asleep for a while. Dad sits at the table, reading. Later Mum comes over to me, removes the wet towel I've wrapped around my hair. Sits behind me on my bed, I lean back, she's clean and warm like me. The smell reminds me a bit of childhood and soap, but not like the soap we had back home. I close my eyes, she dries my hair, rubbing it gently, separating it strand by strand. Takes my comb and pulls it really, really slowly from root to tip, so carefully it doesn't catch and pull out any hairs, as though each were so precious. Just like before in our bedroom at home.

'Such strong, shiny hair,' she says. And then, after a pause, 'I'll get you some rosewater.' And then, 'You've grown so unbelievably beautiful.'

She kisses my neck.

'I'm very proud of my daughter,' she says, so quietly I can only just hear her.

We're enveloped in a mother-daughter cocoon. I want us to be alone. I consciously blur out Rami and Dad and

146

my aunt. It works. When you practise. And I turn to Mum and hug her and feel so at one with her, as if I were small again, even though we both know that's not how it is any more.

It's so cool. Dad's going once a week to work for Laura's mum. He's so happy. He whistles all day long. Ridiculous that it's taken us this long to get here. Perhaps it could've saved all that trouble with him. Another lesson learned.

Went to the letter box today. No letter as usual. But it has to arrive someday.

The boy who stood up for me in front of Mona is called Paul. Kind of unremarkable, quiet. But he likes to read. Comes over to me at breaktime. And says, 'Can you tell me more? I have no idea either. But at least I know that.'

That pleases me. But it's too much, too soon. To tell someone about it all, someone I barely know. I hesitate.

Laura's been watching us, comes over and hugs me. And says, 'It's hard for her, she's not told me anything yet either.'

And I say, 'I can't right now. But I'd like to some other time.'

13

Accompanied Dad to the centre that's dealing with our case.

A new official. 'Why are you here?' And so it begins. 'No, we can't tell you how long it will take. I know absolutely nothing about your family.' He clearly had no idea about our story.

A couple of stupid questions; we'd been here before. Dad got angry. His blood rises quicker every time. He can't bear these questions any more. He can no longer see me operating as his constant mouthpiece, he's trapped in his own bubble of speechlessness. He can't escape it. Or his own skin. I can't either. But it's me that has to deliver his irate words to the officials. And I see those stern faces and keep making up lies, changing his remarks into friendly, grovelling words because if he behaves as he does with me or Mum, we're going to get thrown out. That's my fear, anyway.

'Are you crazy?' Laura asked me when I told her about it. 'You can't change what he's saying! He's the adult, not you!'

When my father doesn't manage to make himself understood without me, I'm allowed to get involved in the conversation. I grant myself permission.

Rami keeps asking to go back to Laura's. That wasn't part of the masterplan.

Sometimes Paul joins us at breaktime. But Laura barely ever lets him speak, so he rarely does. I think it's a shame.

Markus has found the old PlayStation and it still works. Rami's going to be over the moon, even if there are only a couple of old games for it. No assassins for him; just a few car chases.

Markus wants to give it to me in person, Laura says. As if his sister can't manage to hand the thing over. I'm a little bit excited. But just a bit.

Sabina came to school today with her hair a different colour. Red. Laura squealed in envy because the colour was so vibrant. And hers hasn't come out that intense for ages. Despite the bleach. I helped with the bleach and, well, what can I say, we're no hairdressers like Sabina's sister, who uses Sabina as her guinea pig. Her hair looks healthy and shiny too. Laura's doesn't. In some places, she didn't go blonde, more of an orangey-brown. Even after hours. And we burned her scalp. And we had to spend ages rinsing it out. And afterwards there were splashes of the stupid dye everywhere – on the bathtub, the shower curtain, the handtowels, even on the tooth mug. Our hands and Laura's throat and ears were covered in red marks like some sort of contagious skin disease. Bright pink nails. The bathroom looked like a slaughterhouse. And Laura's mum was livid; she could've given my father a run for his money. Where her house and interior design are concerned, she's mercilessly strict. But that's all. Some parts of Laura's hair are now so brittle it snaps off. If Sabina's sister ever needs anyone else to practise on, we're ready and waiting. Anytime. Promise.

Mrs King clearly doesn't like bright colours on young heads. She's made at least three stupid remarks today alone. That's quite something for Mrs King. She only really passes comment when boys wear trousers where their crotch starts at their knees. But she's right about that. I don't know anyone who doesn't look ridiculous dressed like that. Even if they've got the cutest bum in the world. Just looks like they're wearing a poo catcher, like they've not managed to get to the toilet in time. Laura calls them 'nappy trousers'. Sabina adds, 'full ones'. We like those other trousers, really tight. Dark. The ones that show off your whole leg.

Markus arrives at school wearing dark, tight trousers like that and, seemingly disinterested, hands over the rucksack with the games console. Three games to go with it, still in his hand. 'I can tell you how they work?' he says, a question mark hanging at the end.

I instantly turn away. Forget to thank him. 'I still wouldn't get it,' I squeak, and make my escape.

'Hold on, wait,' he calls after me. 'You've forgotten your games.'

If only I could dye my hair a chocolate brown at least. Then I'd look a lot more like the others. Brown with lighter highlights. Then I could make out I'd just been on a really, really long holiday to some exotic destination. Sometimes I'd love to pretend I've simply been here for ever.

Had a strange dream last night. I was going somewhere with Laura, then with Laura and Markus, and then later on, just with Markus. We looked for Laura but couldn't find her. It was night and we stood outside on the street,

Markus and I. I can still remember how I was suddenly close to him and thought his hands looked beautiful. Those hands that I've seen loads before and that sometimes have impressively filthy nails. Thick, black rims, like Rami would be proud of. And somehow he came even closer to me, but I wasn't scared at all. He placed his hands, complete with black-rimmed nails, on my shoulders and it felt good, almost better than when Laura does it, and my belly felt hotter than a kettle; I imagined steam whooshing out of my ears. And then came a really loud, persistent whistling and it took me ages to realise it was my alarm clock.

Been feeling all over the place since I woke up. Still like it after a shower, even now I'm dressed. Reach for my shoulder under my jumper where he touched me in the dream, the skin feels like it's glowing. Can dreams glow on? I think so.

Sitting on the bus later on, looking out across the rainy landscape. Behind me are two boys. At first I don't listen, but then I can't help it because they're so loud. They're talking about Jessica, who was nothing special last year. 'No boobs, no booty,' says one of them reproachfully as if it was Jessica's goddam duty to have prepared her body on time.

'But now!' says the second. Jessica has clearly been putting in some effort. They make a bet, who will be the first to shag this finally ripe Jessica.

Shagging sounds revolting. Makes me feel sick. Then I turn around. They're a bit younger than me. What Jessica has invested in boobs and booty, they must have splashed on acne. And a bit more spent on their hair, plastered down with something akin to glue. I hope Jessica tells them where to go.

On the way home, I ask Laura how Markus is.

She looks at me strangely. 'Why are you asking?' she wants to know.

And I say truthfully, 'I'm not really sure.' But I don't tell her anything about the dream.

It's absurd that someone can think that dyeing their hair is going to change everything. Your whole being.

Laura's annoyed because Sabina's copying her; Sabina just wants to be cool like her. But it doesn't really work, because Sabina's a bit too strait-laced and has no wild ideas of her own. And borrowed wild ideas are the most boring on God's earth.

Mrs King keeps kidnapping me. What have I done to deserve it? I've had it with her biscuits. And her melancholy gaze. And her explanations about God and the world, as if I were some sort of savage who doesn't know how to behave. If I came out wearing a banana leaf loincloth or a grass skirt, I don't think she'd be surprised.

Sabina senses her opportunity. Thinks she's cool. So cool she's throwing a party while her parents are away for the weekend. No point even thinking about going. No way I'll be allowed.

'Lie to your dad,' suggests Sabina, who does that quite often. 'Tell him you're staying at Laura's.'

'Waste of time. My dad wouldn't let me do that either.'

I'm hugely flattered that Sabina's invited me at all. Other than Laura, nobody's ever invited me out. I'm slowly growing on the class, like a piece of transplanted skin that can't be peeled off. Cool.

'Then sneak out,' says Sabina. 'I've done that before. Some of the others have too.'

No, I wouldn't dare do that. Ever.

'Don't be so boring,' says Sabina, who clearly now thinks her hair has turned her into the superior rebel.

No thanks. I don't need any more hassle. I'll skip Sabina's party. Even if it is a shame.

So pleased I didn't lie to my parents. It all came out, of course. Everything. Some of Sabina's mum's jewellery was nicked. A really expensive piece. And her mum squeezed every last name out of Sabina. When she called their parents, it became clear that hardly any of them knew where their sons and daughters had actually been.

'That's absolutely impossible,' said Paul's dad indignantly. 'My son was staying with his friend Nikolaus.'

'But Nikolaus was at Stefan's,' said Nikolaus's mother.

'What? Stefan was with his girlfriend Anna.'

'Anna was at Laura's,' said Anna's mum.

'Laura was at home on her own the whole time,' said Laura's mum.

That much was true. The one person who is given so much freedom they don't need to lie, sometimes chooses to stay at home. Even if there is a party.

It all ended in a huge scandal. Sabina's not allowed out partying for ages. And the others have all been grounded for different lengths of time. It's a bit like a lucky dip; when it comes to punishment, you never know which straw you're going to get.

I know I'm the one with the least freedom and would get the greatest punishment if I did something forbidden. But I don't want to lie. One part of lying is concealment. And I hate hiding things. When you lie, you have to keep tabs on so many things so that the truth doesn't start rolling like a pebble from the top of a mountain, that picks up bigger and bigger stones and by the end, turns into a landslide. And then the trouble starts.

The vampire has made a scene with Laura because, apparently, she calls him too often. When he's in the mood, he calls her as often as he likes and Laura never complains.

And then he sends her messages, telling her how to dress. Not so fucked-up, prettier, skirts and so on. Laura complied a couple of times and didn't feel right. I could tell. It's just not her; without trousers she feels vulnerable. She kept tugging at her skirt.

I know how it feels. I have to wear things I hate, too. When I'm in them I just want to disappear so nobody can see me. You're wearing something you don't want to wear and everyone else thinks that you're choosing to make this fashion faux pas.

Before I was friends with Laura, right at the beginning when we first got here, I had a hideous brown leather coat. It was cold, it'd been snowing and we had no warm clothes, nothing at all for the cold weather, not even warm shoes. Shoes are heavy, boots even heavier. If you take shoes for four people, you have to carry them the whole way. I got lucky with some new winter boots here. I got some fairly nice furry ones from the clothing bank. They looked hardly worn. I was so incredibly happy someone hadn't wanted them any more and I could have them instead. But then my luck ran out: the kids' jackets were all too small for me. Stuff for children is often like new because they're not worn for long. Disappointed, I tried to squeeze myself into a red anorak because I'd already spotted that there was only one other item in my size. Just that brown leather monstrosity, with shoulder pads. I looked like a narrow wardrobe. The leather was lined; I never froze in it. That's true enough. But the coat was for an old lady. It smelled of old lady. It had definitely belonged to an old lady.

'Look how beautifully it's made,' said my mum, trying to cheer me up as I stood tearfully in the doorway the first time I had to go out wearing the monstrosity. 'Well-stitched, good fabric.'

'I don't care,' I wept. 'I look like an idiot.'

'Chest infections look even worse,' Dad said, and that was the end of the coat discussion.

Every day that winter, I felt embarrassed. Every single day. I felt like some fairy tale character, who's actually a person who's been bewitched. Like in the story of the seal skin worn by a mermaid who's desperate to live with people. Or the Frog Princess, who was actually a noblewoman and sorceress but had been cursed to wear a frog skin. Just not at midnight. And I didn't have a kingdom to reign over either, not my old country, nor this one. When I took the revolting leather skin off, I was me again. Just like in the fairy tales, I longed to burn it so I would never have to transform into it again. Was so happy every time I stepped into a heated room.

I don't want Laura to feel even an ounce of that, even if she's doing it to please the vampire. That's not right.

'Don't do it,' I said to her. 'Wear what you like.'

'You can talk!' she shot back. Laura doesn't like any criticism when it comes to the vampire. She gets all extreme. 'You told me you're not allowed to wear trousers. Even though you like them. So? Are you wearing them?'

I went quiet.

Laura bit her lip.

I know she doesn't want to hurt me. And I know I'm trying to show the vampire in a worse light than he probably is. Because I'm jealous. All the time.

'You're still my best friend,' she added quickly. 'I'm allowed to criticise you too, aren't I? Exactly.'

'I'm scared you prefer him to me.' I said finally, finally, *finally*.

Laura laughed incredulously. 'Why would I?' she says hugging me tightly. 'You're you, and he's him.'

I was so relieved. Really shouldn't carry stuff around for weeks on end. The longer you stay quiet the heavier it gets and then it all blows up. I reckon.

'Are you still coming over this afternoon? We'll make some food then chill out in front of the TV.'

Of course I wanted to. I nearly always want to go to hers. At Laura's, time flies. There's always something going on. Markus, or cooking with her mum or just hanging out, completely and utterly relaxed.

＊

After dinner, we lie in Laura's room, watching TV and chatting. We're so close it's like she's my sister, like she's a part of me. Her skin feels like mine, the same temperature. We hold our hands up, they're just about the same size, same length. My skin's a little darker. When we link our fingers together, it looks like a collage or a fashion photo.

'Why did you make friends with me?' I ask. I need to know. I have the feeling she didn't just find me. She was on the lookout. I imagine. Until I arrived.

'Because I know what it's like,' says Laura.

I don't get it. I look at her, baffled.

'Because I know how it is when you don't fit in. It's crap.'

'It is. Really crap.'

I turn onto my side, take her arm and lay it across my shoulders like a thick, warm shawl. Like armour. I turn back over, facing the other way. Without speaking, we know what the other is thinking.

Sometimes speaking just isn't necessary. Causes more damage rather than offering something worthwhile. Laura knows that too. She's silent. Our breathing falls in time. We inhale together and exhale together. A warm breeze on my neck. She smells of peppermint, of chewing gum, and the hint of sweat. The sweat doesn't smell. I hardly know anyone whose sweat doesn't stink. We lie there snuggled up together. Even better than with Mum. I watch her lava lamp, the green blobs of oil floating up and down, slowly, drowsily, sinking to form bigger lumps until a green ball forms again, rising upwards.

Behind us, the TV's on. We don't hear it.

The TV murmurs in the background, weaving an irregular carpet of voices and snippets of music and guns and screeching tyres. I could just fall asleep. My eyelids are heavy but I don't want to. Want to lie here, staring at the green lamp, awake. And silent. It's a beautiful silence, completely different to my parents'. A silence that connects, scatters no question marks or exclamation marks. Always the mystery and concealment. I hate it.

At this moment, I hate it.

'Can I stay here?' I ask.

And Laura says, 'Of course.'

We catch the bus to school. On the way there, I've got a funny feeling in my tummy. Grow more uneasy the closer we get to the concrete building.

Laura laughs at me. Tells me I shouldn't worry. Why do I always worry? Completely unnecessary. Honestly. Her mum made an extra call to the boarding house for me. And if my parents had been really worried, they could've called her mum.

I really want to believe her.

The bus stops at the entrance. I look out the window and spot a small commotion in front of the gate. Several teachers. Waving their arms around, shouting. Hungry for some action, the pupils mill around, gawping.

Then Paul from my class comes over and taps me lightly on the shoulder. Kind of pitifully. And gives me a strange look and says: 'I think that's your dad.'

But honestly, I'm so disappointed with Laura. She left me right in it. Just abandoned me. The whole day, every breaktime, disappeared. It's so not fair. In hindsight.

So. I'm standing there like I'm stuck in mud. Both feet, ankle deep. I need superhuman strength to lift my left foot, move it forward and place it back down. Then the other one. It's just the hardest work, those few steps to the teachers. I glance back at Laura. She's vanished. Slowly I approach them.

Mr Bast's there, and Mrs King. And a couple of other teachers. I don't know most of them. And they're all yelling at each other. 'Please calm down,' Mrs King tries again, her thin voice rising above the uproar. 'Please calm down, let's go inside and talk it over. OK? OK?'

And in the middle, my father. Raging like a monkey. Standing there shouting. And of course, not in German.

His head is pomegranate red. Sweat on his brow. Looks terrifying and also so incredibly ridiculous in his out-of-place shirt and his worn-out shoes. I pity him, yet at the same time I'm dying of embarrassment. I don't know which of these feelings is worse.

'Dad,' I call to him. 'Dad, what's wrong?'

And he spins around. And looks at me. And in that first instance, he's relieved.

Stops shouting. Drops his fists. Then he storms over to me. Where have I been, where on earth have I been? He's been sick to death with worry. 'You traitor! You monster!'

And while saying so, he raises his arm and slaps me.

At first, I don't even realise. Only notice how my head suddenly flies to one side and I'm no longer looking at him or the teachers but the bus stop and the street. And then, the stinging. And I don't start screaming until later, when he thumps my arm. I'm gripping my school bag as if it could lift me out of the situation like a hot air balloon and I could float away with it, over the school and the fields beyond.

And then they all jump on him at once and hold him back and pull me away, and we're both screaming at each other like crazy. He fights like he fought in the war, lashing out in all directions and bellowing like an animal.

'Please, Dad, stop it,' I keep shouting. 'Please stop. Or we're all going to get into trouble. Please. Please.'

A police car arrives, its blue lights flashing. I sit on the steps in front of the entrance, my plait has come loose and my hair falls across my face in wide panels. A black curly screen. I'm still clutching my bag. My biology teacher still stands protectively in front of me.

I see them twist my father's arms behind his back, bundle him into the car and drive away. In the car, he sticks his head out towards me and continues yelling.

I can't believe all that actually happened.

'Do you want to put your bag down?' Mr Bast asks me quietly.

That evening they bring him back to the house. Everyone stands at the fucking windows, in the hallway and in front of the house, watching who's being delivered by the police car. Like a fucking parcel. My father's made sure we have an audience, gawking at us like idiots. Just like this morning.

My mum meets him, crying at the front door. Rami's wrapped around her leg like a chain, wailing the whole time. My mum falls into his neck. I stand behind them. Nobody's interested in how I am. I'm sorry. Very sorry, even.

My aunt is the only one who hasn't left her post at the window. She has to wait for the moon and the stars, which won't emerge in the darkening night sky without her. She hones her night vision.

In our room, we sit around the small table. Mum smiles a pained smile. Offers around tea. She's got nothing else. Dad and I sit opposite each other. I'm trembling. I hold onto the table so nobody notices. My knuckles have turned white. My father's shaking too. His eyes are red. But his hands are completely still. The cup he's holding hovers motionless in front of his mouth.

And he says, 'If our application is refused now, it's all your fault. Yours.'

I instantly start to cry, although somewhere in a distant corner of my consciousness, I feel that what he's saying is wrong. I didn't force him to make a scene outside school. I can't help it if mean old Mrs Boss didn't pass on the message from Laura's mum, meaning my parents didn't know where I was. And of course they were out of their mind with worry. But despite all that, it's not my fault!

My mother smiles and smiles, strokes his forehead and soothes him. Speaks to him with the voice of a nightingale, no, the voice of a dove, cooing and grovelling. Telling him I hadn't done it on purpose. A mistake, yes, but not malicious. Laura's mum *did* call. The landlady just didn't tell them. Nothing at all. And I feel bad. I didn't know. I didn't mean this to happen.

And in spite of all the tears and guilty feelings, I also feel like I'm standing a step further away than before.

If our family were a house, I'd now be on the threshold, one foot in the garden, the garden gate in sight.

And he shouts some more, bangs the cup on the table and shakes off her arms from around his hunched-up shoulders.

'We thought something had happened to you! How could you do that?'

I sob. Really badly. Between snivelling and trying to catch my breath, I only manage a few jerky words.

'I didn't mean for it to happen. I didn't know! I thought you knew where I was!'

And Mum and Dad both look like I've said the wrong thing again. I'm just trying to explain! I've already said how sorry I am.

'The fact we didn't know where you were is one thing,' Dad speaks as if I were an ill, stubborn cow. 'Worse still is that you wilfully chose to spend a night away.'

'Everyone here does it,' I sniff. The anger that had sunk deep into my belly throughout the horror and anguish with him and Mum begins to rage, like a dragon that takes a while to warm up.

'*YOU* don't! You are not one of them!'

'Here it's completely normal!' I yell. The dragon breaks free, without a backwards glance at me. My head and my belly are so hot I fear the words will shoot from my lips as forks of fire. 'You will never understand it. Never! Never!

If we're not allowed to stay here, then it's not my fault! It's yours! *Yours!*'

Mum positions herself between my blazing fire and Dad. Poor Mum. One hand on my shoulder, the other on Dad's arm, skewered between us. 'Please, Eli,' she says. 'She doesn't mean it like that. She means it differently. Please. Otherwise the police will come again.'

'How else could she mean it?' roars my father. 'She's just like your sister! You know what happens to girls like her. You know what such wantonness leads to!' And he turns to my aunt who's still sitting by the window. 'They end up like that one there! Couldn't you have brought your daughter up better than her?'

At that, my aunt gets up, stands very straight, very quiet. And appears to grow. And grow. So big it seems she's touching the ceiling. Her black shawl falls noiselessly from her shoulders onto the floor. Like dark snow. In contrast to his shoulders, hers are straight. She squares them. No longer looks like a cat. More like a cobra set to attack. Nobody moves.

And my silent aunt opens her mouth and speaks very loudly.

'You don't need to talk to me about decency. You're to blame that I have to live like this. And you know it.'

There's a pause. My father holds his tongue.

Then Amina says wearily, 'You know what you're

guilty of doing to me and my husband. You don't need me to remind you. You *betrayed* us.'

She turns back around. Slumps into a heap, picks up her shawl, gathers it tightly around her shoulders, faces the window again and returns to her tireless moonlight task.

Despite the horror of the day, I feel electrified. This untouchability that surrounds Amina lit up for a second. I sense a story behind it, the dimensions of which I can't grasp, but I feel it's suddenly founded in concrete. There's a story behind the veil that cloaks her whole past. We have two pasts. One pre-war and another post-war. A shared past with cities and villages, work and sport, with gardens, schools and pretty streets full of cafés and restaurants, with cars and buses and holidays. Everything harmless, normal, the day-to-day. And then comes the dividing line drawn by the war between all of that and us, behind which our unshared pasts begin. Those experiences that each of us has lived on our own, incidents that have only been witnessed by that one person and that only they know about.

14

At school they're whispering about me far more than before. Because of Dad. Thanks, like, really. Even those who were indifferent before are joining in now.

'Next time it'll be someone bringing a bomb,' says the prick from the class next door. 'They just don't get it.' And the two scumbags nearby laugh.

Laura purposefully walks past them, arm linked through mine, head held high. She says to the prick, 'Is there something wrong? What's your problem? Piss off!'

I've still not confessed to her how desolate I felt when she disappeared outside school. Just wasn't there any more.

During lunch break, Mrs King came into the classroom. In her tight-fitting black dress she looked elegant, yet also like a scarecrow. Although perhaps more crow than scarecrow. Alert, stern and gaunt, dressed in black with her head jutting forwards and a long, pointy nose.

I really don't understand why she doesn't like crows; they're her nearest relatives. I say that to Laura. She snorts, loudly. She's going to call her 'Crowface' from now on. I just know it.

So Crowface walks into the classroom, head leading, dark eyes peering in, followed by her shoulders, then her whole body. She takes me to one side. Laura tries to stay with me. She asks Laura to leave. I feel a bit sick. Laura waves to me then turns to the window. Mrs King steers me out of the classroom. There's a lady standing outside who I've never seen before.

'This is Ms Wischmann,' says Mrs King and smiles. She looks more sinister with this smile on her face than when she's being strict. At least the strictness is real.

I take a step backwards. The woman doesn't look like she's from the police. Nor like one of the officials I've seen when I've been to report to the authorities with Dad. But how do I know what all the different officials look like here? Ms Wischmann's wearing a red dress. A pretty red. And green sandals. Her toenails are painted green. And she's got a double chin, too. And a pair of red glasses on her nose. I try to size her up.

'Ms Wischmann would like to talk to you,' says Crowface.

Ms Wischmann says, 'Hello,' and puts her hand out.

I take it and also say, 'Hello.'

She looks me straight in the eye, her handshake is just right, not too firm, not too weak. I shake her hand and think, Not again. Not a repeat of all those endless questions, filling out paper questionnaires, my whole history from before, and then all over again, every repetition becoming more and more absurd, my past becoming less and less comprehensible, because every time I repeat it, I see it through the eyes of the person opposite me. And those faces reflect a lack of understanding. And pity. And a look of, 'Oh my God, the things she's saying, the poor thing,' or, 'I hope she's not spinning me a line.'

Mrs King repeats, 'Ms Wischmann would like to talk to you.'

But I don't want to talk to Ms Wischmann. That much is clear.

'The bell's about to go,' I say hopefully.

Crowface shrugs her black shoulders and says, 'I'll give you a free period.' She walks into the classroom behind me and closes the door behind her.

Ms Wischmann and I stand alone in the corridor.

She beams at me, as if standing with me in an empty school corridor is the best thing in the world, and says, 'Come with me.'

It's not a question.

I follow her towards the closed school nurse's room. No school nurse today. She spends a few moments hunting through the enormous keyring to find the right key, trying several in the silver lock.

She clearly wants to talk to me about my father. I could strangle him. But I know I definitely don't want to get him into any more trouble. I'm just not sure how to do it. I don't want to lie. I can't lie, anyway. I'll blush, start sweating and won't know where to look. No. I won't lie. Worst-case scenario, I just won't say anything. I feel awful.

She bids me into the room with an inviting gesture. I see the bed and the dark patchwork blanket on top, stare at the pattern and prepare to escape to my fairy tale world. I stretch out my hand and touch the wall, imagining it's a tree trunk. Can almost hear the leaves rustling above me, shadowy in the shade of the thick tree canopy. Bird call.

'Madina,' she says.

'Sit down,' she says.

And then again, louder, 'Madina!'

My hand isn't resting on a tree trunk but on a school wall. It's cool and dry.

Ms Wischmann settles in behind the school nurse's desk, crosses her legs and smiles at me. 'I want to talk to you about the incident last week.'

She shuffles forwards, expectantly.

Obviously. What else would it be? I cross my arms across my chest, she unfolds hers, purposefully relaxed. I get the message. I'm meant to believe I can trust her.

'Dad can't help it,' I say. And I stare at the floor. 'He gets very worried about me.'

'I think so, too,' she says. And with that, she takes the wind out of my sails.

I ride home on the bus with Laura. We look out the window. The space between us is wider than I thought, and filled with awkwardness. I want to be close to her and vice versa, but there's all this other stuff. Stuff that keeps getting in the way. She tries to ignore it, I know, and I try to get over it, but sometimes we just get stuck in it, and it won't go away. Sometimes it's knee-deep, sometimes as big as a mountain. It's not down to us. Really. We do try. And we get there, time and time again. But this other stuff is unpredictable. Keeps slipping from our grasp.

Laura's mum has invited me over as always. Today should be pizza day. Whatever. I'm not hungry.

I get home. The cat runs towards me and rubs herself on my leg. I have no energy for her today. In my head, the conversation with Ms Wischmann is still whirring around. Her suggestions, that aren't really suggestions but instructions. And the knowledge that it's going to be really hard to convince Dad of this necessity.

I hear my parents arguing while I'm still on the stairs. I stand outside the door. Lean against the wall in the hallway. A neighbour comes down the stairs. 'You're in for it now,' he says smugly.

My parents get louder.

I could open the door now. But I don't. I listen.

'That's not how it works,' shouts my father. 'Not in my house!'

'Like you've got one.' That was my aunt.

'You shut your mouth!' My father's voice gets louder. He's suddenly hoarse.

My mother coos. How is that all she can do?

'It won't happen again. Rami will look after her.'

'You don't mean that,' says my mother.

I feel my anger rising.

What?! My father must have completely flipped. Rami, the little squirt! My hand is on the door handle, I want to storm in there and ask him if he's really serious, that my seven-year-old brother is meant to look after me, the kid who can't even tie his own shoelaces without them coming undone, causing him to trip and fall flat on his face! Who cries because he's not allowed to go to the cinema like everyone else!

But something holds me back.

I lean towards the door.

'This isn't why I left! I've not gone through all that just for this!'

'Just be grateful it's all over,' my mother says. 'Be pleased we're here in safety. In safety, don't forget that.'

'So she can lose all decency?! A young girl, staying out all night!'

173

And mother, softly again, 'She was worn out. They studied a lot that evening.'

That's very sweet of her; the homework book actually never came out my bag at Laura's. As usual.

'In houses where men sleep!'

At first, I didn't get what he meant. As I pieced it together, I flushed hot, then cold. Markus. All this because of Laura's brother. I'd laugh if it weren't all so awful. If it weren't so damn unfunny.

'Who's going to want to marry her?'

Marry? I could throw up, right here.

And my mother: 'She's still so young. Why are you thinking about that now? She's still got time.'

Thanks, Mum.

'This country will break us. You're forgetting everything that was. You're forgetting what's good for us. It'll all end badly.'

'We'd have all been killed,' says my mother. 'Be grateful we're here. Please, come to your senses.'

'I won't stand by and watch while my daughter, here . . . here . . .'

He chokes, lets out a sob, struggles for words.

Outside I'm struggling for air. Now. *Now* he'll say it. And I know, I know, it's the end for us, and I don't want it to be the end. He's still my dad. I used to sit on his lap. I trusted him. I love him. More or less.

But he doesn't say it. He sighs, stamps his feet but

doesn't say the words I'm so scared of. Nothing about his or my honour.

'And when she goes to ruin, it'll be me that's to blame,' he says, suddenly quiet.

I press my ear to the door and feel the splintering varnish against my cheek.

'I brought her here. It's my fault.'

'But you're not to blame for the war,' my mother says.

'But it's my responsibility. Everything that happened. Everything that will happen.'

Mum says absolutely nothing else. Maybe she's put her arms around him; when he next speaks his voice is muffled as if he's speaking into her soft belly, nestling into her bosom, into her arms.

'It was a mistake. We shouldn't have left.' And then a long silence.

And then Mum again: 'You saved us.'

And Dad: 'For us to go to the dogs here. My mother at home and us here. I don't know what's worse. And if they throw us out again and she returns ... Returns as she is now, or worse still, as she'll *become*. As one of *those* girls. A disgrace.'

And Mum: 'What are you talking about?' Her voice is suddenly harder. 'What is wrong with you? You never used to speak like this back home. Why now all of a sudden?'

'Because. Everything. Here. Is. Different.'

Dad's words leave his mouth like gunshots. I'm compelled to think of bullets that cause particularly gruesome damage to the body's tissues. 'Bodily tissues,' my father would say every time we were faced with bloody flesh, mangled skin, white, broken bones sticking out, before we'd go in to disinfect them with alcohol, bandaging bones together, sewing stitches. And someone had to hold the injured person's mouth shut, so nobody heard them yelling in the cellar. I know how a man's mouth feels as you use all your strength to press it together, the hard stubble under your fingers, the dry lips. These bullets force their way into the body's tissues and bloom like horrifying steel flowers with sharp edges, opening up in the moisture. A deadly bloom. He used to be quiet. He never raged, never yelled, never didn't trust me. No, he believed me back then. He was the surgeon and I was his assistant. He was proud of me. And I was proud when I didn't need to go and be sick behind the house.

And Dad continues shooting. 'Because we're foreign here. And we have to stick together. Because otherwise this land will devour us. Who are you without your past? Only a nobody has no past. All right? Enough.'

And Mum tries her dove calls again. She's untiring in her attempts. Alarmingly tough, as tough as he is, but different. 'She's fighting like a hero for us. She's helping us. You can trust her.'

'Of course she's helping us! We're her family!'

'Exactly,' says Mum. 'Can you make yourself understood without her? I can't.'

Dad mumbles something I can't hear properly through the door.

'Trust me. Trust her. She knows this country better than you.'

And my father shouts again. 'She knows nothing! If she did, she wouldn't have done it! From now on, the rules will be different, before it's too late. No, let me go. Leave me alone!'

I hear the chair push back, scraping across the floor.

I move quickly and step back from the door. As a precaution.

He takes three loud strides towards the door, each one making the room shake, flings it open, trying to flee from my mother's eyes, from her sweetness, and stands before me.

I hold his gaze.

He clears his throat. Mum stares, her nails digging into the arms of the chair.

I draw together all the strength I have in me. As I inhale, I feel myself summoning everything I've got. I. Must. Do. This. Now.

'Dad, I need to talk to you,' I say.

He grins, half aggressively, half helplessly. 'Oh, but of course.'

And my mother in the background, 'My love, please!'

He says, 'Come on in.' He takes my hand as he used to do when I was small and we'd walk along the road together. He takes my hand like he did when we hoisted our rucksacks onto our backs for the first time. I don't pull away. He leads me into the room. We sit down at the table. My aunt immediately leaves.

'School wants to organise a meeting for us all,' I say.

'Do they indeed? Do they want to call the police again and have them drag me away like a criminal?'

'You freaked out. What else could they do?'

'*YOU* could have behaved yourself.'

I don't rise to it, just as Ms Wischmann's advised. 'We have to talk to them, Dad.'

'I've told you already. If we now get refused . . .'

'Dad, school wants to help us. They sent a woman who'll mediate for us. To avoid exactly that, getting into trouble. We just need to go along with it. Please.'

My father erupts like a volcano. In a split second, even his head turns lava red. His lips are suddenly glowing. He leaps up. 'I'm not talking to some woman I don't know about my daughter's behaviour,' he starts again. 'There's absolutely no need for a meeting to talk about stuff that doesn't concern anyone else.'

'Oh, come on, Dad. When you hit me in public, it concerns everyone. That's how it works here.'

My father begins to orbit the table where I'm still sitting, faster and faster. I'm not sure whether he reminds me more of a shark circling its prey or an aeroplane that's lost control.

'Not in my house! Not in my family!'

'Dad,' I say. 'If you want us to have our own home again, then this is what we have to do. If we don't do it, they'll press charges. And, Dad, that's big trouble. You know that.'

Mum wades into the battle for the first time. 'Madina's right. Just to prove we're managing all right and complying with their rules. Please. Think of us all.'

He sighs. 'There will be consequences. For you too, Madina. Oh yes. I'll go and see her, I get the point. But I will be taking action. This will not happen again.'

'Dad,' I say, 'it's just a meeting. We've had so many useless meetings. This one here's useful.'

He mutters something. But I can tell he's not a volcano any more, but an ebbing flow of lava, its pressure waning. 'You never used to speak to me like this,' he says. 'You never used to argue with me.'

'Dad, I still love you,' I say, and the tears begin to fall, because I feel a chasm open up between us, a gap I'm not sure we'll ever manage to close.

He stands there, leaning on the table, and drops his head. I feel the tears running down my cheeks, dripping onto my throat. Mum does nothing. Not because she doesn't care. She just doesn't know what to do.

He breathes deeply. Rubs his chest as if he's in pain.

His head is still flame red. 'I won't let some woman tell me what I can and can't do. Not several women, either,' he finally says.

'You can't do that here.' It's all been moving in the right direction, sort of, but it slips out before I can bite my tongue, 'That's not how it works here.'

He shoots me a look that makes me feel numb, right down to my belly. Wild, hateful. He's never looked at me like that before.

I swallow. Force myself to look at him. His lips tremble. And his hands.

He inhales deeply, waits until his hands are back under control and says, 'They've stolen you.'

I want to be on my own right now. I'm sitting under the stairs next to the cellar door, knees pulled up under my chin. My bum is freezing. It smells damp. I'm so tired, my eyelids keep drooping. I'm sitting down here but I'm not scared. It's not like the cellar we used to sit in while the bombs fell. I'm sitting here on purpose.

I want to feel that this cellar is a different cellar, not ours. The bomb cellar where Mum and I would tell Rami fairy tales so he'd fall asleep quicker. I'd tell stories, crying at the same time, just so quietly, it was silent.

I sit there, feel my legs go numb and my arms begin to tingle. My back pressed against the wall, my diary on the floor next to me. At the moment I carry it with me all the time, like a witness.

I've no desire to go upstairs. Perhaps they're looking for me. Whatever. At some point they turn out the light in the hallway. Sometime afterwards my mother calls my name. Not my father. I don't answer. And a little later still, I hear cautious footsteps, so I pick up my diary and stuff it under my jacket so nobody can see it. I shuffle forwards in the half-light and see Rami coming down the last flight of stairs towards the cellar. Fear is written all over his face, he's forcing himself to take each step down. With one hand, he's holding on tightly to the bannister, the other hand is balled into a fist in his pocket. He makes himself keep going, one step after the other. It takes so much effort I can see a sliver of his tongue poking out between his lips. I've told him so many times not to do that. He ought to be careful. Not run round with his tongue out. He promised me. But he doesn't realise he's doing it. If he trips now, he'll bite his tongue.

'Hi,' I say, so he can find me and no longer fear being alone in the cellar, because he doesn't know whether he's actually alone with the stale air and the strange shadows that are cast by the upturned boxes at the entrance. I like these shadows; even when the light's on, I'm still concealed.

He raises his head and looks around for me, the tip of his tongue disappears. Still looks like a rabbit in headlights. And when he finally spots me, he pulls a serious face. Eyebrows knitted together towards his nose, corners of his mouth turned down. Just like Dad does. He's wearing a colourful T-shirt with a bear on the front and short trousers that were once long. He sticks out his skinny arms and says forcefully, 'You're coming with me.'

I can't help laughing. And say, 'No way.' But he's welcome to join me if he likes.

He briefly considers his plan of action and says, 'Nope. You've got to come with me. I'm the second most important after Dad and you have to do as I say.' Looks of untamed pride and untamed doubt fight each other on his face. Great, eh? To finally be the second man of the house. And so full of shit when nobody responds to it.

'D'you know what?' I say to him. 'I'll come. In half an hour. Sit down and wait with me, OK?'

'I can't,' he says. 'Dad'll get cross.'

I get it. I know how it feels when you're scared of Dad's outbursts, which, for all their rarity, really pack a punch. He throws pots and pans, furniture, anything he can lay his hands on, he rages and roars. Afterwards he's usually remorseful and we collect all the broken bits and pieces together. Before the war, he'd buy beautiful things for us to replace the ones he'd destroyed. He was truly sorry. During the war he hardly ever lost it.

It had to be something really bad to raise his blood. It's like that in war, you know what proper trouble is. You brace yourself and hold it together the whole time. But at such cost to your nerves that afterwards, it only takes some trifling thing to set you off.

'Sit down, Rami,' I say.

Despite coming over to me obediently, as a compromise, he remains standing, imperious. His lower lip trembles, he'll start crying next.

'Fine,' I say. Stand up, pick up my jacket and diary.

'What's that?' asks Rami.

'Nothing,' I reply. 'Let's go.'

If my little brother keeps scampering after me like some stray dog, I'm going to flip.

It feels so good to go wherever I like in my wood, my own private journey. They can't deny me this outlet. When I exit through the door, creep noiselessly past my aunt's stony stare and the wolves beyond that, the darkest of dark woods begins. Where the wolves don't go. I daren't go in either. But you can't cut through the wood without crossing this darkness. I've often climbed tall trees, gazing out across the vast grey-green surface of the tree canopy. The wood extends left and right. I look out onto a sea of green, light and dark. Delicate shoots, old, withering boughs covered in moss. Treetops wafting like meadow grasses. The wind blowing through their hair. In the distance, on the horizon, a flat plain and behind it rises a

rust—red mountain peak. The sea isn't far beyond. But to get to the sea, I have to take a step into the darkness. And I know I can't do that.

My Laura-anger has completely blown over, leaving only Laura-worry behind. I miss her and feel more and more uncertain.

Mum and Dad discuss who's going to come to school. He speaks, she doesn't. Mum obeys.

Amina watches on scornfully. 'I wouldn't drop my child in it.'

Mum winces. 'I'm not dropping my child in it.'

'What, just like you didn't drop all of us in it?' my aunt asks. 'I won't hold my breath.'

And Dad storms over to her.

I quickly step between them. One more brawl for this family in this country would be one brawl too many.

'Dad!' I shout. 'You can't do that!' And I turn to my aunt, 'Please go outside.'

Amina actually does so straight away. She listens to me! I follow her and close the door firmly behind me.

'Don't provoke him,' I say. 'Do you want us to get kicked out?'

She just looks at me.

'What is wrong with all of you? Are you all mad, or what?'

'You have no idea,' she whispers. Her face freezes abruptly, as suddenly and strangely as when she heeded me before.

'Then tell me once and for all, what is going on? Can't you see? I'm trying to help us all. Mum says you married against your father's will. That can't be the only reason for all of this.'

'You really want to know?' Amina asks. 'Why don't you ask your parents? Your dear old dad.'

'Because he only ever bullshits me.'

She looks a bit happier. 'All right, fine,' she says. 'If you insist. But I'm warning you. You'll have to work through the consequences on your own.'

I have no idea what that means.

'First off, I marry the man I love. What a crime! And then ... then your father starts playing the hero. The selfless hero. The whole shebang. And draws attention to all of us. They weren't stupid. They knew who was being treated in your house. They knew who was coming and going. But it was me and my husband who paid the most for it. All because we're related. That was enough.' She shrugs, half helplessly, half angrily. 'They were looking for *him*,' hisses Amina. 'Your father, not my husband. But they only found my husband at home. None of you were there. That's why *you're* still alive.' Her voice sounds completely

185

different. Gloomy. The smile extinguished. 'And now, with my husband dead and me a wanted person, just like your "respectable" father, he makes out I'm worthless. And there's nobody here to protect me. My husband paid for your dad. And in return, your father spits in my face.'

'My dad wouldn't do that,' I stammer. I really want to believe my words. I want to be certain. But right now, there's a huge difference between wanting to be certain and actually knowing. And what I start to glimpse in between, makes me most nervous.

'That's all I'm going to say.'

'I'm trying to understand. Maybe . . . Maybe it can all be sorted out. Can't it?' Our teacher said you can resolve everything. If you're prepared to talk about it and change. I so badly want to believe everything can be resolved.

Amina laughs. A spine-tingling laugh. It's been a long, long time since I heard her laugh.

15

Ms Wischmann has dressed up for the occasion. This time a green dress with red tights and red earrings. A bit like the Christmas tree that stood in the school entrance during December. No face looks good with a double chin. But somehow hers looks nice. All homely. And the red lipstick suits her. The opposite of Crowface's figure of mourning. Mrs King really is in mourning. But I won't make fun of mourning. I wouldn't want anyone to make fun of the fact I miss my grandma. Missing someone like that always makes you the butt of jokes; people notice how needy you are. Most people here are surrounded by people they love, so they feel safe.

We sit at the table in the nurse's room: me, Dad, Mrs King and Ms Wischmann. Mum stayed with Rami.

Ms Wischmann has brought a flask and dishes out tea. 'Milk?' she asks with a tinkling voice that you could mistake on the phone for someone my age. 'Sugar?'

My father thanks her politely, takes sugar in his tea and sits there so nervously his restlessness overspills onto everyone else. Despite all the worry, I breathe a sigh of relief that Mrs King hasn't brought any shortbread biscuits with her.

Ms Wischmann explains that in this country you are not allowed to use corporal punishment. It's forbidden. My father must accept that and, as long as it doesn't happen again, there will be no charges. She understands it was out of concern. But still.

He tries to say something, but she doesn't let him distract her. This is absolute torture for me; I have to stop interpreting what she is saying to him and start interrupting her with his words.

But Ms Wischmann remains polite, smiles kindly. I wish I could be like her. 'Worry is absolutely understandable. But violence will not be tolerated. We have to keep an eye on the situation.'

I'm under observation, for a while at least. She goes on, saying that this can only be in his best interests, ensuring his daughter is OK.

My father's face is like a concrete wall. Grey and impenetrable. Having not been able to get a word in earlier when he wanted to, he now has nothing to say. As punishment. It's a shame Mr Bast isn't here. At least there'd be another man around the table.

'Your daughter has a good life here,' Ms Wischmann says. 'Perhaps this change is difficult for you. I understand some of it will seem incomprehensible to you.'

'I understand well,' my father says. 'I understand.

I just don't believe it is good for my daughter.' And then he adds, 'You haven't seen what I have seen. You haven't experienced what my daughter had to experience. You believe she is safe here. I prefer to be cautious.'

'But you can't task your son with looking after his older sister.'

'Of course I can. If you understood me, you wouldn't say that.'

At the end of the meeting, Ms Wischmann was at least convinced that my father is as stubborn as a mule. But I'd told her that much before.

On the way home, he kept clearing his throat. Just before we reached the house he stopped suddenly. 'I'm sorry I hit you,' he squeezed out. 'I didn't mean to react so heavy-handedly. I'm sorry.'

Me too, Dad. Me too.

I'm so worried Laura doesn't like me any more. Because she's now seen how my dad behaves. Like a madman. Laura's mum hasn't invited me over again. I can't bear it if Laura's not there. Can't bear it if her mum doesn't want us to be friends any more. And if Laura's not there, Markus isn't there either. And then I've got nothing here. Don't even want to consider that.

I'm off to look for the cat.

Laura wasn't as absent in school today as before. Every day on the way to school, I'm filled with so much Laura-worry my tummy hurts, to the point that I have to go and fart in the toilet before the bell goes and then again at breaktime. Please don't let Laura be angry.

Dad is such a loser. Really.

Don't want to write any more. Sitting downstairs with the cat. Can't be bothered with anything.

Still can't be bothered. Whatever.

Rami's been whinging all evening. 'Madina's not doing what I say,' he snivels around the place. 'I don't know what to do.'

And Mum smiles her mummy-smile – I could just slap her for it – and she says, 'You've done enough already.'

'But if something happens to her, do I get the blame?' wails Rami again. 'It'd all be my fault.'

'No, my love,' my mother says. 'You won't get the blame.'

He doesn't believe her.

He's not a big fan of it all either. Dad's ideas are ridiculous. This'll be fun, I think to myself. It's all going to go wrong. I wonder who will screw it up: me, Rami or my parents.

My bets are on Rami.

Hey! Laura sat with me at breaktime again.

Ms Wischmann says she wants another meeting. My father's refusing. I'll go on my own. He can't stop me.

Went with Laura to the vending machine. We drank coke and chatted a bit.

Mum and Dad keep arguing about me again. Most of the time I walk out. Sometimes I can still hear them from outside in the yard.

Hear how my father yells. 'I still have to function. And I still have to function for the others. I'm still their father and your husband, and I'm in charge!'

And sometimes my mum argues back. Questions why he's so stuck on the past? Says she doesn't recognise him like this!

And he roars louder because he's not used to that. 'Because we don't belong here! Look around you, see how they treat me! Like I can't do anything. Like I'm useless!'

And Mum says, 'They've taken us in.'

And Dad, 'It's charity, given against their will!'

'You wanted to come!'

'I wanted to survive!'

It's so miserable. Miserable. I desperately need Laura, if I don't want to end up drowning in a senseless rage.

Mrs King asks how I am. Not great. She reminds me to speak to Ms Wischmann. Actually, for a change, that's not a bad idea.

Wonder whether Laura is cool with my trips to Ms Wischmann, me running off to her every couple of weeks. Hope so. She thought my visits to Mrs King were definitely not cool.

I'm waiting for Laura to ask when we'll meet up again. I don't dare. But Laura doesn't ask. When she talks to me, she has a look on her face like someone walking a tightrope who really has to concentrate. We're all balancing along, each on our individual tightropes. I'd love to wobble over to the platform where her tightrope leads. But she moves over towards Sabina. Who's just waiting for her. That hurts.

Paul uses the opportunity and sits next to me more often. I like him and it's good not to be totally alone, but it's not Laura. I barely know him. He makes me nervous.

I write Laura a note during German. Mrs King is so absorbed she doesn't notice, even though I'm sat in the front row. I don't write much, just: *I like you.*

Laura takes the paper, waits agonising minutes before opening it. Reads. Smiles. Scribbles something then pushes the crumpled piece of paper back to me. On it there's a smiley. And: *I like you too, you idiot. Don't beat yourself up.*

I'm so relieved. Take the paper and stick it in my bag as if it were a love letter. Whenever I'm doubtful again in the future, I can look at it.

We both know, Laura and I, that something's happened that's too big for us to understand. But I hope we can work it out together, step by step.

Laura's mum has invited me over again, but I'm not allowed to go. Perhaps Laura can come here. I'm so sad now I just don't care what it looks like here.

No such luck. Laura's not allowed here either.

We're allowed to go for a walk together. Tomorrow. Halfway between Laura's house and ours. Adults are so stupid. All of them. Rami has to come with us and is already whining that we're too fast for him. Exactly. I'll be counting on it.

'Does your brother really have to come?' Laura asks as soon as we start out. Incredulous. Annoyed. Disappointed.

I'm so worried. Her voice doesn't sound good. She sounds like the rumbling in the clouds before a storm. So quiet from a distance, but dangerous nonetheless.

And Rami says all importantly: 'Yes, of course.'

Laura shrugs. 'If you say so,' she says to me. But I can tell she's really pissed off. 'Let's go, then.'

We walk quickly, cross over the field and head into the wood. There are gnarled, moss-covered roots you have to avoid or clamber over so you don't trip. Rami doesn't manage it and keeps falling over. The first time I wait for him to get up. Only the first time. As the path bends, we can't see him any more. Behind us Rami's shouting; I pretend I can't hear him. At some point the calls become quieter.

'This isn't right,' says Laura. 'Either you bring him or you don't, but this is wrong. He'll get lost in the wood.'

I say nothing. Walk on. Crying. She doesn't notice.

'Come on,' she says. 'Let's turn around. I don't fancy spending hours searching for him.'

I'd love to lock Rami in a storage room with Crowface and throw away the key. I'm going to sleep now. Good night.

Laura's begged her mum millions of times. She's allowed to pick me up and take me out somewhere. She's not allowed to come in. Like it's life threateningly dangerous. What does Laura's mum actually think? I've been living here for two years.

I meet Laura at the front door. She stares. She's truly out of place. The hideous house, the knackered walls, the screaming children. The veiled women. One of the men grins at her. Probably well-meant. Perhaps not. Murmuring voices in the yard reminiscent of the Tower of Babel. The smell from the main kitchen wafting down. Laura chews her lip. One of the recently arrived young men sprawls near the kitchen door and whistles at Laura. She winces. I take her hand. And stand between them. Between everything that could horrify her and everything that represents my day-to-day.

'Get lost,' I say to him. 'Disappear.'

'I don't want to come here any more,' Laura says as she's leaving. 'It's horrible here.'

I've never felt as filthy and unsightly as today.

Came home this evening and lay in bed, pulled the blanket over my head and tried to sleep. Skipped dinner. Didn't want to see anyone. Not even Laura. If Rami talks to me again today, I'll beat him black and blue.

Right. I'm on my way to school. Rami needs to keep his distance. The stupid arsehole.

Class drags on. I'm not listening. The teacher picks on me and I don't know how to answer. Mr Bast looks at me sharply and threatens me with a minus grade. If it makes him happy. I wait impatiently for breaktime then I grab Laura and clear it all up. I'm not standing for all this not-talking-about-it any more.

Laura looks defeated. 'I'm so sorry,' she says, over and over. 'I'm so sorry you live there.'

'Better than on the street,' I reply.

'But only just,' she says with a small smile. 'You could move in with me. We've got space for you.'

'And what do I do with my parents?' I ask. 'I'll stick them in your junk room, shall I?'

My father keeps pretending it's all OK. Nothing is OK.

The next letter from Grandma has arrived. I don't comfort Dad this time. Besides, there's little reason to comfort him; Grandma's fine. And Grandpa too. She even visited my dad's brother, my uncle, in the city, went to the doctor's and saw friends. No bombs at the moment. The battles are taking a rest. It's quiet in our village and the neighbours are taking the opportunity to mend the damage again. Roofs are patched up. Windows and doors fixed. Those with money replace the glass in the windows. Those without make do with paper and plastic. That's nice. I think of our garden, our goats. The flowers and fruit trees that look different to the ones here and smell different, too. Only the goats smell the same. Goats smell the same worldwide.

When I hear from Grandma, it always gets to me how much I miss her. Other than that, I've not thought much about her recently. That feels very unpleasant. How could I forget my grandmother? Her laugh, her food, her hugs, her eyes, so dark like those of a turtle, a sea turtle. Unwittingly, I imagine how grandma would sink majestically into the depths of the sea, swimming with elegant arm movements through the silvery fish shoals, floating in the deep blue with her shell on her back, wearing her flowery dress. I have to laugh and can't get the image out of my head. The more detailed the image, the less I want to imagine it. It's like when someone says: don't think about pink elephants. And then what do you think about? You got it.

Rami's just the deputy arsehole. The principal arsehole is clearly my father. But it's easier to be cross with Rami. Why should I be fair when the others aren't?

Surely Grandma would know what to do. Grandma would know how to talk to Dad. And to Rami. I so badly want to console myself knowing my grandmother could unravel this tangle of problems and roll it all neatly back up again. I wish she was here, so much it takes my breath away.

Laura thinks it's ridiculous. No young people our age are as attached to their grandmother as I am. To her, it's laughable. Of course, she can see her grandma every day if she wants. Not the other grandmother who lives further away. But one of them at least. I've only got one grandmother. My mother lost a parent early on and lived with relatives until her father remarried. And Mum often told me the new wife didn't like Amina at all. Right from the off. Because she was so beautiful. Beautiful, proud Amina. And the new wife wasn't as pretty. Unlike her sister, my mother made an effort to make the stepmother finally love her. A whole lot of effort.

Sometimes I want to stroke her and say, you've worked so hard for love, Mum. Be happy. We're all here. And we love you.

But then it's sounds silly, so I don't.

16

Laura's just about back to normal. We're spending most of our time together again. A bit more cautious, like two ice skaters on new ice. But I've still not discussed it all with her.

'Are you scared of my dad?' I ask her as we come out of school.

She hesitates. 'Nah, not scared.'

'But?'

'But nothing.'

'Laura, I can tell.'

A strange look comes over her. 'D'you know what, Madina . . .' she says. 'I can't stand it when men scream and shout and all that. I just can't stand it.'

I nod eagerly. 'Neither can I,' I hurry to add. So as not to lose the connection with her. My palms are sweaty.

'You have no idea,' Laura suddenly says.

And I think about how I've never told her about Mori, or the patients, or the disfigurements or the dead. Because I wanted her to be a beautiful chapter of my life. A beautiful, clean chapter in a beautiful, clean country with a beautiful, clean future. And even now I know I won't tell her about any of it now. What's the point? It won't change anything.

'My dad,' she begins to say and then stops again. 'All right. I'll tell you. But not here, OK? I'll tell you at home.'

'I'm not allowed to come over without Rami, remember?'

'Oh crap! That's so tedious.'

And I start worrying she'll say she's done with it all. That she's off. But Laura's cool. Even when she's scared.

'You know what? Let's go to McDonald's after school. No, even better, let's go an hour early.'

'If we get caught, my dad'll kill me.'

Then we remember PE's cancelled tomorrow. I've not given the letter to my dad yet. Or translated it. I just won't. Simple as. And if he asks, I'll translate it wrong. It's his own fault, he should be learning German. He thinks I'll be home around four. He can keep thinking that.

We sit in McDonald's. I keep glancing out the window, jittery in case someone walks past who might tell my parents. Mrs Boss, perhaps. She savours opportunities like that and she's been holding it against me that outsiders have been in and disturbed her. She should be overjoyed I've not dobbed her in because there's never any soap or loo roll, or told them the cook keeps taking our food home.

I'm so nervous I can't even manage half my burger. The sauce has dribbled from between the two halves of the bun and splattered on the table. I dabble my fingers in it. Doodle squiggles and spirals. Then I dunk my elbow in my artwork by mistake. Great. A red stain on my white top.

Laura's not as relaxed and chilled out as usual either. But not because of me.

'I told you it wasn't always easy for us, didn't I?'

I nod.

'Not easy is an understatement. It was really, really awful,' says Laura, making a real effort to keep calm. And I notice her lips and chin trembling. And as she begins to speak, her voice trembles too. 'My parents got divorced, yeah?' Her voice gets higher and squeakier.

I think back to the photos in her house, each with a part missing. Chopped off where her dad once was. But by cutting him out, he's not really gone. Rather the opposite.

'It was all so shit, Madina. So shit.' She crumples her burger packaging. Tears the paper tray liner into tiny pieces like confetti. And then I see the first tear roll down her cheek. She lets her red hair fall across her face, partly defiant, partly ashamed. I don't move.

'Mum yelled. And Dad pushed Mum through the

glass door.' Laura huddles into herself, shrinking. 'Splinters of glass and blood everywhere. You've seen the scars on her belly . . . everywhere . . . And Markus called the police.' She's speaking in fits and starts, quicker and quicker, as if the air she's breathing won't suffice for what she has to say. 'And Dad was given a restraining order. I don't know. I just don't know what would have happened if he . . . if he . . .' She bursts into tears.

I awaken from my stupor and hug her really, really tightly. She presses her head to my chest, constantly shaking it from side to side as if trying to deny it all.

'Let's go outside,' she sniffs. 'They're all looking.'

So they are. Even the girl on the till. I grip her hand tightly, just like Dad used to do to me. Laura lets herself be led out, like I've often let Dad lead me. When someone presses hard enough, they make you believe they know what's what. Even if that's not always the case. For instance, I only know how to get us outside, out of the light, away from the watching eyes. After that, I haven't got a clue. But I don't let that show.

'Mum had an affair,' whispered Laura. 'With the neighbour. Everyone knew about it when it got out. And the neighbour was married, too. But he didn't end up divorced. It was all Mum's fault. That's what the whole village . . . the whole village was saying. And they all gossiped about us . . . And I was still only little. Nobody wanted to be my friend . . . nobody. Or Markus's.'

We're sitting behind the restaurant. Using a box as a mat. Next to the bins. It stinks!

'If Markus hadn't been there, I'd have been finished. I wasn't invited to a single birthday party. Like I had some contagious disease! Dad filed for divorce. Mum got the house. Put her all into it. He wanted nothing else to do with us. I don't want to see him any more either. Markus meets him every now and then. He feels bad that Dad was arrested because of him. But what else could he have done? I can still see the blood sometimes, when I look at the glass door. Even though it's not there any more. Mum's drinking more and more, you've seen all the empty bottles, haven't you? Sometimes Markus has to carry her up to bed. Sometimes she cries and I have to calm her down.'

Laura takes a long pause. I wait patiently. Sometimes you just have to be patient.

'The neighbour moved away with his family. Everyone called my mum a slut. None of them called *him* a lech. None of them. And we stayed. As did the gossip.'

Laura sweeps her hair out her face and looks at me. Her make-up's all over the place, not just where it was before.

'I can't stand any man on the rampage,' she says. 'I can't bear men who do that, you know? That's why I ran away when your dad ... But then I felt so scared ... I couldn't do anything else. I'm so sorry, I just couldn't ...'

I rub her back, her shoulders. I recognise that fear.

I know that feeling; being naked in the snow, completely powerless.

Laura clings to me like a monkey. I don't think she was ever as close to me as she is now. Her mascara mingles with snot on my jacket. And I say to her what Mum and Grandma always say: 'It'll all be OK.'

Of course, that's rubbish, because what's happened can never be OK again. But that feeling, that can improve. The now. When it's something so bad, it can't move into the past because it's tied too tightly to the present. Continually interrupting this safe new life, hanging around like an uninvited guest. But it interrupts less and less. With time.

I must not cry. I'm in caring mode. I have to be the one that's strong, oozing calm. I will be here for Laura. I rub her back again, her body relaxes, as heavy as a sack of cement. She leans into me and sobs and sobs. She's warm, soft in some places while in others, I feel her bones, her pointy shoulders, boring into my chest. I stroke her hair, her cheeks, as if she were a child and I her mother. As if we were family. It feels like we've transformed into a snuggly pretzel, but a very sad one. I like her warmth on me.

And I'm horrified that someone here would do the same as back home. I know what happens when someone loses control. Entering the neighbours' homes and destroying everything that isn't nailed down. Beating people, killing people. Distorted faces, arms that are raised and commit actions that can never be made good again. And I know the remorse that follows. After the intoxication of violence. They often turn meek and whiny, whimpering apologies. They fill your ears, saying they hadn't meant to and they had no choice. And I knew it even then: of course they had a choice. My dad made a choice in the end, too; he wouldn't join in. You can make that choice. It works.

Mrs King and Ms Wischmann remind me about our meeting. Like I could forget. It's ringed in red on my calendar. As red as Laura wishes her hair was, like Sabina's actually was.

'You had a call,' Mrs Boss says, lying in wait for me in the hallway, like a ghost in the half-light. 'A "Markus" wanted to speak to you.' There is a strange undertone to her voice. Perhaps it's because she copped a load of bother from the school for regularly not passing on important messages. Ms Wischmann threatened her with consequences. I love her for it. Ms Wischmann's turned into my mobile shield that even works at a distance, if required.

Why did he call? My heart does a little flip. I'm not sure if it's from pleasure or horror.

The meetings with Ms Wischmann always put me in a strange mood. It's like she understands everything. That's creepy. Nobody understands *everything*, probably not even God. If he even exists. But God is definitely not Ms Wischmann. I consider telling her about the wood and the stars and the ship. I don't tell her anything about the bombs.

Grandma wrote yesterday. She made some cakes. And the new neighbours visited her for tea. I would so love to see her again. Hug her. Or at least just hear her. A voice says so much more than simple written words.

I wake up far too early, go quietly outside. Everyone's still asleep. Walk barefooted through the cool grass, sparkling with dew. Feel the damp earth. Look down into the valley. Already a few cars out and about. This is me-time. It's lovely to sit out here writing my diary without anybody looking over my shoulder. I'll write to Grandma later on, tell her about Laura. That I've found a friend. A real friend. I want to tell her I'm almost as grown-up as she is, because I can comfort other people well. And that I'm proud I can hold my nerve in certain situations. I learned that from her.

That evening, Mum wants me to go and fetch Dad from the community room because her back's aching from cleaning the stairs again and it's late and she can only relax when we're all back. She never gets to sleep otherwise. Rami's in his pyjamas lying snuggled up next to her under the blanket.

I shuffle off in my slippers, down the stairs. The lightbulb's gone on the ground floor. The darkness doesn't scare me like it used to. I only notice it once I'm back in the light. Before I'd have been worrying about it long before getting there. The evening news is on TV. Normally it's noisy and smoky in here. The men sit around the plastic table talking. It's like a guesthouse. Women rarely enter.

Dad sits a little off to one side. He doesn't want to come back. I can tell from his face.

'Mum's waiting,' I explain.

'Why didn't she send Rami?' he asks.

I'm suddenly so full of rage and stare at the TV to bite my tongue. The next headline. Blue lights. Sirens. A distressed presenter in front of a smoking underground station, cordoned off with a red-and-white striped tape. People with singed hair, blood on their faces, screaming, people crying, people lying on stretchers and laughing in shock, firefighters. Some of them call out.

'Where's that?' one of the men asks.

'Must be far away. It's safe here,' replies another, soothingly.

But the city they name isn't far away. Not beyond the seven mountains, not over the sea. It's in Europe. It's even in our new life.

My knees buckle. 'It was here,' I say to my dad.

People running around screaming. Police officers wearing gloves come into shot, their fingers visible in the close-ups. A young woman wearing torn trousers sits crying on the pavement, her naked knee poking out. She doesn't need anything, she sobs. But her boyfriend's still down there. An old man with a burned face is being treated. He waves his arms around, hindering the first aider. The veins on his hands are dark blue. Behind him I make out a body covered in plastic. I'm pleased not to be able to see more than just the plastic. The old man with the burn on his face looks like he's got a cartoon head on a human body. Somehow it looks ridiculous. Loud confusion, uncomprehending looks. They aren't familiar with this. We are. Only now do I realise the pictures are from this morning. It's light. The shadows cast by the people are still long. It's around ten a.m.

Dad gets up with a jerk.

'What are they saying? What are they saying?' they clamour.

I begin to sweat, my legs give way.

'We're going,' Dad says. 'Ask someone else.'

I can't tear my eyes away. They show photos. Blurred CCTV images of men with rucksacks. They zoom in. My stomach churns. One of them reminds me of the weirdo from the second floor. But the image is shaky, black and white and you don't see his face from the front. And he's wearing a baseball cap. The weirdo never wore one of those. And I've only ever seen him in colour.

It all turns black before my eyes. I sag to one side. Don't pass out completely, just a bit. Sit slumped against the wall.

Dad comes over to me and touches my forehead. It's damp. 'Quick, get a towel and water,' he calls.

One of them presses something horribly cold onto my neck, water runs between my shoulder blades.

'Dad, that was our old neighbour,' I whisper.

And Dad snarls at me, 'Definitely not! Get that out of your head! And don't get involved!' And he yanks me up and drags me up the stairs.

'Never say that again,' he says outside our door. His voice sounds scared. 'It wasn't him. Gone. Finished. Over.'

Sitting with Ms Wischmann, shuddering from a crying fit. Sobbing so hard she no longer hands over tissues. The box she placed so welcomingly on the table is almost empty. I bury my nose into the soft, perfumed tissue. Maybe it's all my fault. Maybe it could have been stopped. Maybe I should have said more to the police officer.

Ms Wischmann lets me cry until I'm done, and says very gently, 'You can't be sure it was him.'

'No,' I sob.

'So then,' says Ms Wischmann. 'If you want to say something to the police, we can do it together.'

'Why didn't Dad want to talk to me about it?'

'He's worried about you. That much is clear.'

Do you think the weirdo could have something to do with it? I want to ask, but I don't dare.

She seems to feel it. She smiles. And says, 'Your dad wants you all to start a new life away from danger. He just wants you to be safe. That's all.'

Ms Wischmann is like a fine red line that separates the unbearable from the everyday. When I talk to her, everything seems so much easier and clearer. And every time, I get back home and realise it's not clear or easy.

There are rumours and whispering in the hostel. Clearly nobody else other than me has made any connection to the weirdo. That soothes me. But somehow, the safety we all searched for here has been shaken. We're all away from home. Some insist we're still better off here than at home. Others sit in their rooms crying. Mrs Boss walks around the floors looking as if she's expecting to find bombs under all the beds. She's going through everything, opening wardrobes, lifting mattresses. Of course she finds nothing.

Laura comforts me at breaktime. I've not really told her anything, I'm just very quiet. She phones Lynne. She tries to cheer me up. I love her for it.

Lynne's coming to eat ice cream with us. Markus might be coming, too. And Rami of course. Christian the vampire, however, isn't. While I'm pretty pleased about it, Laura's disappointed. Yesterday I was forced to listen to twenty minutes of telephone drama. The whole way home. Her begging. And his lazy excuses. Saying that, arguments like these are so much better than the ones at home. With Laura, it's like some absurd, unreal normality descends. When we're together, it's all somehow more bearable. Markus adds a pinch of unpredictability. But just the right amount. One that doesn't make me worry, only quickens my pulse.

Rami worships Markus. Sticks to his heels like he's stuck with superglue. And it obviously doesn't bother Markus. Not yet, anyway.

'Why is your hair so long, like a girl?' asks Rami. 'Aren't you embarrassed?'

Markus laughs. 'Long hair's a sign of freedom,' he says.

Rami listens, his mouth gaping.

'Why would it be embarrassing to look like a girl?'

'Because girls can't do anything,' says Rami.

'Girls are great,' replies Markus.

Lynne laughs into her iced coffee and a blob of squirty cream flies off the top and lands on the table, Rami sticks his finger in it and licks it off. I blush.

Like so often over the last few days, I just wish I could swap places with Laura. Just be her. Have her family, her house, her past. But I know that's not how it works.

Small afterthought: Actually, I don't want to swap with Laura. She's currently crying her eyes out over Christian the vampire. He's not getting in touch. Won't answer the phone. He's stopped messaging her too. And Laura's in despair. Christian's always there when we're together. Sits on the table, revises with us for exams, comes on walks. All she talks about is him. Every second word is 'Christian', and every third, 'arsehole'. And every fourth sentence, she declares, 'But I love him so much!' It's like an illness. You can't prevent it even if you want to, just like throwing up.

Laura's got it bad. She's irritated with everyone. She's starting to write Christian off, but she's not quite there yet, I hope we can soon go back to the two of us again. Just us two. And perhaps a sliver of Markus.

Laura's absolutely hopeless! No sooner is the vampire off the scene but she's blatantly flirting with someone else! He called twice yesterday alone. Wanted to invite her to the cinema.

'Pick me up from school,' she suggested to him. And whispered to me, 'So I can show him to you.'

I just rolled my eyes. I already kind of know him. From before, when I was allowed to visit Laura. Nothing special. Unremarkable. But friendly. One of the quiet ones who always blurs into the background. I remember him sitting between two others boys on Markus's sofa. Messy black hair. Washed out T-shirt. He coughed. Made out he was some great smoker, puffing desperately on his cigarette.

That was when Markus was christening his new PlayStation. With his mates. Laura and I were trying to do our homework in the room next door. It was so loud in the other room we could hardly think. Later on, Laura had had enough, jumped up to have a go at them. As she got to the door, she stopped, turned around and asked whether it wouldn't be better to do it together. I gave her a questioning look. She knew I always try to avoid any sort of confrontation. She smiled her Laura-going-into-

214

battle smile as she leaned against the door frame, one leg jauntily crossed over the other.

'Markus has a new classmate who's here, too. Don't you want to see him?' she asked.

'I'm not sure,' I replied.

It sounded like we were planning a visit to see a dangerous animal behind bars. Markus's friends were as threatening as an iguana or a sloth. Hung around saying nothing. And when they did speak, they mumbled so slowly, like they had a mouthful of chewing gum. And when replying to Laura, slower than ever. Sunglasses, zits and piercings, with the following pattern: the more zits, the more likely the shades and piercings. Back then I was already curious about Markus's mates. But I'd never dare go in.

'Come on,' pleaded Laura.

There were two options: let Laura go in and soon after, hear her voice through the wall, murmuring and laughing. Or go with her, hide behind Laura and steal glances over her shoulder into the boys' room. Tough choice.

So Laura decided for me, grabbed my arm and dragged me across the room.

What does Laura see in him? He's really nothing special.

My fear of meeting the weirdo again is fading. They don't mention it on the news any more. People quickly forget.

Laura's addicted. She's now eyeing up the next guy because the first one didn't get in touch! Does she really need to work her way round all of Markus's friends? I think that's disgusting. OK, I admit he's got nice hair. And no metal in his face. But that's still not a good enough reason.

17

'D'you know what?' I say to Laura on the way home from school. 'Perhaps Lynne has an idea about how I can persuade Dad to learn German. He has to. It won't work if he can't speak German.'

And she looks at me dubiously. 'I don't think you can force him to.'

'I don't want to force him. I just want to know how Lynne's dad did it.'

'He wanted to live here.'

'Mine does too. I know he does.'

'But not voluntarily.'

And I get terrifyingly angry at her because she's so dense and just doesn't want to try and understand where I'm going with this.

'You really are thick sometimes,' I say, and I jump up and with full-on rage, kick my bag lying on the bus floor. I walk down the bus towards the driver and get off before Laura's stop. I've got to walk several kilometres now. Or wait ages for the next bus.

She taps her head at me through the window. I flip

my middle finger at her. Well done! That was just what we needed right now.

I get home late. Mum's running around, green in the face. Where have I been? And why?

'Mum, it's just forty-five minutes, for God's sake!'

'That's not the point.'

Wonder if Laura's mum worries as much about her children as my mum does. Whether she has such catastrophic thoughts with Laura at the epicentre. Probably, she loves them a lot. Just differently to how our parents love Rami and me. Less uptight. But I try not to get upset about it. The circumstances are just different.

Dad comes back up the stairs, shouting before he gets to us. 'Come here, come here,' he yells. 'A letter's arrived. Come here, Madina, what does it say?'

We all shoot out like bullets from a starting pistol. Rami first as he scurries between us, then me, and finally Mum and Amina.

He waves the letter. I take it from Dad's hand. Is this the long-awaited letter? The letter with the right stamps and the right sender? With the right answer? With the answer we're all waiting for?

'What do they say, Madina?' Dad splutters, sweat beading on his forehead.

The glass is half full or half empty. It's a letter from

the office handling our case, but it just says they'll make a decision within the next four weeks. That's it. And they enclose a note from Dad's new caseworker. Who's clearly only just getting into it and writes that the application looks very strong and that Dad is not to worry. He continues, saying it's crystal clear that Dad's life would be in danger at home and that he shouldn't be deported. Suggests there's not much now that can go wrong; Dad just needs to be patient. It's still not a reliable answer. But somehow, it's a weight off our shoulders.

Dad runs around with us in front of the house. He twirls me around, and then Rami, like we were little again. It's raining outside. He splashes with us in the puddles and laughs and laughs, throws his head back and lets the rain fall on his face. I see his Adam's apple bobbing up and down as he laughs and shouts. The neighbours stand at their windows and watch. Mum too. She's crying again, but laughing at the same time, and she waves at us. Amina stands behind her.

Her face is expressionless.

I know everyone is envious, although nothing is certain yet. Any one of them up there would swap places with us in an instant. I feel so proud because we're suddenly something better than them. Then I'm ashamed of my reaction. But not straight away. Pride is like a jar of honey, thick, sweet and dense and the shame a pinch of salt. We almost belong now. We've finally, nearly, actually made it.

We're in the midst of arriving. The sky is a pinky-red. It smells of lilacs and damp garden earth.

Can't sleep. Imagine having our own flat. Where Dad can finally relax. When it's all finally good. I stare out of the window. The night is long. I turn in my bed like a chicken on a spit. Until dawn arrives and the first rays of light appear on the horizon and the birds outside begin to sing. Oh, you little birds, I think. I'll miss you when we move out.

In a few hours, I can tell Laura.

Mrs Boss calls as I go past: 'There's a letter for you!'

'Yes, I know,' I say. 'Thanks. We got it yesterday, from your husband.'

'No,' she replies. 'Another letter.' And gives it to me.

I look at the sender: Grandma. I'm pleased to hear from her again. But my head's full of school. I've got so much to do if I want to have time for other people; I have to sort out the argument with Laura. So I hand the letter to Dad and head outside to study. As I run back upstairs to fetch a book I've forgotten, his face has fallen.

'What's wrong?' I ask.

He replies, 'Nothing. It's all fine.'

I really want to believe him, and I've no spare energy to dig any deeper. And I have to study. 'What does she say?' I ask anyway.

'Not a lot,' he says.

'Can I have the letter? Later, when I'm done?' I ask. He says, 'Not now.'

Seems strange. But hey, probably just another of his crazy ideas. I'll worry about it later. I take my book and leave the room.

Spent a very pleasant afternoon with Laura down at the lake in the woods. Feeding fish. Swimming. Lying in the sun like two lazy turtles, a plastic punnet of cherries in front of us, spitting the stones into the water. Counting the ripples. Skimming small flat stones over the surface of the water – whoever got the most bounces won. The last stone was completely flat with a white vein across it. We skimmed it together, swinging our arms around several times, and on the count of three, we let it go.

We talked about what we'll be able to do once my family can move out. Perhaps move in with Laura's mum. In the basement. Or the attic. Laura hopes so anyway. I don't really think that'll happen. Her mum won't go along with it. We'd be happy if Mum could clean for her at least. Dad could look after the garden again. Laura won't let it go. She said she'll fight for us. Word of honour. I believed her instantly. They had lodgers before when Laura was little. Not because Laura's mum needed the money. But because she didn't feel comfortable alone in a big house. Despite all that, we created this image of togetherness, developing the storyline, like a fairy tale. Sunbathing in the garden. Hosting parties. Cooking. And always travelling to school together. No absurd time limits on our visits. Like real sisters. House sisters. Markus popped into my head. I asked her what he'd make of it. Thought about his forearms, suntanned, with little blond hairs, like Laura. That golden shimmer she has is so unbelievably beautiful. I blushed bright red. She looked at me. Half amused, half angry.

'Do you like him?' she asked me outright.

I went even redder. Probably pepperoni red.

'You're not serious, are you?' she asked. 'You can't be serious.' Laura's very sensitive about this subject, the vampire's going out with someone else. And she doesn't seem as keen on his successor. With him, it's the complete opposite: he calls her and she doesn't answer. 'Markus? My *brother*?'

I couldn't look at her.

She elbowed me in the ribs, a bit too roughly, and I couldn't laugh it off. 'And?' she probed.

'Just a bit,' I stammered.

We went our separate ways at the fork in the road before the house. I walked home, all the way thinking about what Laura said. And I wondered why she reacted so strangely. I've put up with two Laura-snoggers so far. And Markus hasn't even given me so much as a peck on

the cheek. I thought of him kissing my cheek and felt
hotter than that dream I had before.

Everything's weird at home. Too messed-up to write about.
Honestly. They're all insane!

I don't ever get to read Grandma's letter. Instead absolute
chaos has returned. Mum's crying incessantly. And because
she's crying, Rami's crying too. Mum begs me not to
breathe a word to anyone. I have to swear an oath and
promise on my honour, even though she won't tell me
what's going on! It's all so frightening, I start to feel
scared. Only my aunt behaves as usual. Sits, stares, silent.
And every so often, says something nasty. Mum and Dad
sit there, gazing into space. For hours. I'm so happy when
the school bus arrives and I can escape.

Laura asks what's wrong. If I'm annoyed because of
Markus. No, I'm not. I've got other worries besides
Markus. But I'm not allowed to say anything to Laura. I
promised!

Dad's silence grows and grows. It's like a wall between
him and us. Sometimes I think Dad's turned into the
rings of Saturn. We're the planet and he's orbiting us at

a distance, doesn't connect with us, unreachable. Sometimes I think if I go to touch him, my hand will glide through him like fog. I'm always relieved when my hand comes to rest on his shoulder. He's sitting in the mottled grey-black jumper that Mum knitted him years ago. In just a few months, his hair has become as mottled as the jumper, tangled and wiry beneath his fingertips, no more Chipmunk Daddy. He sits there, motionless, staring into his tea. There's always lots of tea in his cup, just as there's always lots of tears in Mum's eyes.

I could kick myself for having sworn to silence. You can't promise something like that. If I'd have known how serious the situation is, I'd never have promised. I can't even tell Laura that everything's been turned upside down and I don't even know why. I feel cheated by the adults. This is all their shit, not mine.

A whole week has passed and Dad's still not speaking to Mum. Barely to us either. They are mad!

Rami can't stand it. He keeps trying to distract the adults. First, he climbs onto Dad's lap until Dad gently pushes him off again. Then he wants to play. Then to have dinner, even though he knows all too well it's not time. Then he shouts at Mum, grins at my aunt and off he runs down the hallway. Or he hides somewhere and cries. Or he visits his friends. Doesn't usually come back until dinnertime and if he's not there by then, there's even more trouble, and he knows it.

Right. I can't wait any longer! Either they tell me. Or . . . or . . . I'll move in with Laura.

I'll move in with Laura. Sounds so strange, that sentence. Had to write it down again to make space in my head for that colossal phrase. I'll move in with Laura. My first thought is wild. Beautiful. And tempting.

My second thought is fear. And I can scarcely think any more. There's a question mark in there: I'll move in with Laura?

And with that question mark at the end, I know I'm going nowhere. Whatever they do, I'm not going anywhere because they're so helpless. What would they do without me? Rami can't interpret half as well as I can. He wouldn't understand even the simplest meetings with the authorities. I do. I know what I'm doing. Even if I'm clueless as to what's going on right now. They're not saying anything. I can't force them to. I can't.

Caught Mum on her own in the room, hugged her so she couldn't escape and pressed myself into her. And as I held onto her, I asked her what's going on. Again, she didn't say anything. Then I felt her shoulders tremble slightly, a barely discernible tremor. Like a ripple on water. The waves broke over me and the arms I'd wrapped around her, until Mum stood there calmly again. Then she hugged me back. We stood there. Motionless, each with our head on the other's shoulder. Time stretched like the dough Laura's mum uses for her pizzas. Then slowly, as the dough was kneaded, time broke through. Then Mum took a deep breath.

'Your dad wants to leave.'

I thought I'd misheard. 'Dad wants to what?' I asked.

I *must* have misheard. Can't believe it. But they're all acting so weird. There must be some serious reason for it, and if Dad wants to leave, it must be very, very serious.

'Leave,' she said. 'He wants to leave.'

Dad was out all day, all evening. No idea where. Good, I told myself during the evening. Yes, good, let him go. Sounds so unreal, like I'd heard it in a film, where someone's dad said they want to leave. Not mine. I don't even know where he's going. How long for. Or why. I don't dare ask. But I'll write him a letter. I've decided. I'll write to him as if he were my diary. Sounds crazy. It *is* crazy. I'll end up as mad as the others if I'm not careful.

At night I walk around my wood. And I know it's not enough any more. I won't solve anything just tiptoeing around the edges. I have to go deeper. I have to find a path that leads further than the way I've already come. The light barely penetrates, individual rays of light between the boughs. The wood is dangerous and you mustn't underestimate it. If I want to get to the other side, to the sea, I have to navigate the darkest labyrinth. I try. But the shadows grow gloomier and I can scarcely see the narrow path before me. My heart's racing so loudly that I wake up.

I understand so little. I want to be alone. I don't go into our room at all, but head straight to the wooden bench behind the house. Facing down the valley. On the left, the car park. On the right, a couple of fruit trees belonging to the farm opposite. The bench is covered with moss, it's wonky and creaks as you sit down. You count the seconds until it breaks underneath you. But it never does.

Dad and Rami are sitting there. Dad's in full flow. He can be very convincing. Right there and then, you want to believe what he's saying. But I know from experience that some of it just doesn't add up. Perhaps it used to. But not here, not now.

'You have to be a big man. The big man of the family. You have to look after them. Your sister. As always. But.

Listen. It's going to be different. You have to look after Mum, too.'

'Why Mum?' stammers Rami, completely bewildered. Then they see me and huddle together like children caught stealing apples.

18

It's Saturday already. Laura's gone away with her brother. I didn't want to go. Didn't want to lie, and wanted to avoid the temptation to tell her everything, finally tell her everything, so she knows why my head's spinning, so she can hug me and I can lay my head on her shoulder, bury my head in her chest, and pretend nothing's happening.

The sun's shining, it's warm. The neighbours have spread out colourful blankets on the floor in the yard and are picnicking, without a picnic. Just water bottles and apples they've collected in the garden. The little kids are shouting. Rami with them. They're all so loud. But in high spirits. I hate these happy cries that are in such contrast to the cotton-wool silence that's been dumped all over us. I know exactly where to find Dad. Walk around the house to the shadowy side where it smells of damp, where nobody wants to hang around. Sit down next to him.

Dad's smoking. Started again. I wouldn't have even realised before. The smell always clung to his clothes, but I'd never see him. The cigarette's dented and looks like

Dad's picked it up off the floor. Don't want to even consider that my dad might be smoking cigarettes thrown away by other people. I sit next to him, my legs dangling like I'm a little girl again. He's staring into the distance. So am I. I know it'll end in a duel.

A bit like before, when we'd have a staring competition, waiting for the first person to blink. They'd lose. Whoever looked away lost too. Whoever moved. Whoever spoke. And I think, Whatever you can do, I can do. I won't budge an inch. I'll stay with you, whatever you do.

We've been sitting here for absolutely ages. He flicks the cigarette away. The butt flies to the floor like a shooting star soaring through the air. He treads on it. Then reaches into his trouser pocket for the next cigarette, as battered and almost as burned as the first.

I head into my wood. And I force myself not to turn back like last time. Deep breaths. Close my eyes. Count to three. Open my eyes again. And on three, I just go. Fast. Faster. Branches whipping my face. Don't care. Run through them. Even though I can no longer see anything. Even though it's so dark, I can't see my hand before my eyes. I run and run, and get the impression the way is shorter than I'd guessed from outside. In the distance, I see beams of light breaking through the branches. No more animal eyes in the darkness. The sound of birds singing again. Far away.

I could have a go at him for being so stupid and fight my battle that way. I could let rip at him. I'm so angry, I'd love to roar at him to piss off, go away, just leave, at least then we'd all know where we stand. How can he do this to us? But when the anger subsides, I'm just a crumpled heap of misery, an anxious heap. With a bad conscience. Perhaps he's going because of me, maybe I'm the reason he's finding it so hard. Maybe. I know it's ludicrous, but that's what keeps running through my mind. I want to go to him. Hug him. Want him to know how much I love him. He clearly doesn't know. Otherwise he wouldn't be leaving.

Nobody has banned me from treading this path. And nobody can. Once I've passed through the door, tiptoed past my aunt's stony gaze and the wolves, the fields of mist begin. From there, it's not far to the sea. Once you escape the mist, you can almost touch it.

But it's not fog creeping across the ground; the mist fields are formed of mist flowers. Long, lightly-coloured stems, large, tubular petals, like white lilies in bloom. A sweet, bewitching scent so I take only shallow breaths. Thousands of mist flowers, emerging from the earth, swaying as I run my fingers through them. As tall as my hips, some as tall as my belly button. When

I walk through them, they disperse into fine wisps of mist that immediately close in around me. You have to be careful where you're going. Otherwise you can become disorientated in the dazzling fog and never find your way out. Fear blinds you ten times more than the flowers, their white mist flowing out of the open, pale grey tube-like petals. They sense the fear. As I push them apart, the flower mist follows my hand, wrapping itself around my fingers as if the plants are trying to ensnare me.

I know there was someone who let out a red thread to guide them back out of the labyrinth, Laura told me about them. Somewhere deep within the labyrinth, a monster was waiting, a man with the head of a bull that had to be slain. I never liked the story. How come the man with the bull's head was a monster? All he had was . . . how shall I put it . . . an external issue. Just like me and my wretched leather coat that had me branded a monstrosity, all winter long. It's often unwise to label something a monster. I always felt sorry for the Minotaur. I'd never have killed it. I'd have helped it to escape, using a lead and muzzle. I'd have fed it properly and trained it instead. Pasta in place of human flesh. Maybe even tofu. There are vegetarian monsters too. Definitely.

I have no thread to tie to anything. It's very quiet here. From somewhere in the empty whiteness comes the drawn-out call of a swan. I can't see any swans. You'd barely be able to see them. Everything white on white. The call sounds sad. But I remind myself that swans always sound like that, even when they're happy. Need to tell myself that a couple of times to make myself believe it.

I have to wade through this mist soup like a swamp. Being careful my feet don't sink into the mire. Mist flowers grow in unstable ground that can give way beneath you. I'm slow. Forcefully wrenching my heavy, sodden boots out of the mud. Sometimes it's better to go slowly. To consider every step. I wish I were better at it. Step by step. That's how I'll get through the field unscathed. And I must vanquish the field if I'm to make it to the sea. The coast beyond the ravine. The ravine still lies before me. Onwards, onwards, I tell myself. And I breathe in the mist and breathe out again, creating two fine clouds. Looks like I'm smoking. The mist envelops me. I mustn't wait too long or it will seep into me, saturate me and I'll evaporate into another veil of mist, without flowers. Dissolving me. Deleting me. I mustn't lose sight of my goal. In here, the stars aren't visible to guide you.

I reach for the stone teardrop hanging around my throat. It's throbbingly warm. I trust that Grandma is expecting me. That thought will guide me instead of the stars. I mustn't forget that the sea lies beyond. And the coast. And at the coast, the ship. My ship. Just waiting to set sail under an expanse of dark blue star-studded sky.

What comes next will be awful. I wish it wasn't all unravelling. But sadly. It is. And I can't talk to anyone about it. I hate eavesdropping. But sometimes it just happens. We've all probably been there. You get into a situation where you can hear and you just can't stop, especially when you realise it's about you. And then it's like you're hypnotised by an angry wizard and can't move, and you hold your breath, and when you're part way in, or rather, when you've heard too much, you're stuck in a dilemma. Can't just walk in and say, 'Erm, I heard all that. All your ugly secrets that affect me too. I *knew* something was wrong.'

But things so often go wrong and our family is infiltrated by all these secrets, or things we can't say, or silences, or outbursts, without ever revealing that at some point, I wearied of it all. At some point you stop coughing because nothing else comes up. Especially when there's so much to do. This Realm of Mum and Dad ceased as my one and only world, and I'm trying to remain in the one place where I can see my life evolving in a way that feels good. But it hurts. And that frightens me. And I reproach myself for not having loved my parents enough.

I arrive home, hear my parents arguing. This is the moment to turn around and leave again quietly, so as not to get caught in the storm of words. Yes, that would be the best thing, to just walk away. But I can't do that. I tiptoe the last few steps, but there's no need to be careful. They're so carried away they definitely won't hear me. I stand still. When Mum and Dad say such horrendous things, it's so hard; I can't bear to listen passively to them.

I imagine they're not my parents, but actors. Some other actors. A play on a stage. A film. A radio drama. Something that has nothing to do with me. I just want to find out how it finishes, this stupid story that has nothing to do with me.

WOMAN: You're still not ready! Where are our documents? And the notebooks? Our language class is about to start. Can you stop pacing?

MAN: I don't need the class.

WOMAN: You're not serious? You don't mean that!

MAN: I don't need the class.

WOMAN: What am I going to tell the social worker?

MAN: I don't need the class.

WOMAN: Be reasonable!

MAN: I've told you lots of times already, haven't I?

WOMAN: But we've already signed up!

MAN: I don't need the class. I'm going to learn the language of war again.

WOMAN: I'll speak to her and you have another think about it. I'll tell her you're sick.

MAN: Go on your own.

WOMAN: Perhaps we can move to the next class, or . . . I'll start now and you can start later . . . Stand still! Look at me! Please.

MAN: I can't.

WOMAN: You're going mad, and driving me crazy too. Just sit down.

MAN: Leave it!

WOMAN: There. Sit down.

MAN: No.

WOMAN: You missing your class won't make it any better for your little brother! You're walking into a trap. They're clever. They know where to stick the knife.

MAN: They don't need him. It's me they want.

WOMAN: They'll take you and you'll both disappear.

MAN: Not necessarily.

WOMAN: You know that's how it works.

MAN: Perhaps not this time.

WOMAN: Really? Are you sure about that?

MAN: No, no I'm not. But you know I can't change it.

WOMAN: You have a choice.

MAN: I have *absolutely* no choice at all.

WOMAN: Hundreds of people die every day in that country. Every morning. Every evening. But I want to live. With you. I want you to live. And the children.

MAN: I haven't decided anything yet!

WOMAN: The fact you're even thinking about it … it's unbearable!

MAN: You know I have to obey *my family*! I'm my mother's eldest son. I have to protect my parents and brother.

WOMAN: You can't make that decision alone! It affects us all! Is your honour worth more than your children's lives?

MAN: What future do they have as the children of a traitor?

WOMAN: They have one here! How is it right that you rescue the old and sacrifice the young? How can you turn around and leave your own children behind?

MAN: It has to be right because tradition demands it. How can I wake up every morning and continue living when I know I'm to blame?

WOMAN: You are not to blame for the war! And you didn't do anything to anyone!

MAN: I'm responsible for everything that happens.

Curtain falls. Play ends. Silence.

I'm shivering. I get the feeling it's all over. My whole life as I know it.

The mist fields reach as far as the rusty-red mountain. I've made it through the mist. I see the sun. The sky. The ground is firm again. Ruddy, porous stone. I wipe the sweat from my face. That was close. That was really close. And I must go on. I'm nearly there. Nearly. I no longer look around. The mist wall remains behind.

Before me rises a mountain, a ruby-tipped summit. Sheer mountain faces. I stretch out my hand: the stone feels warm, like flesh. I walk a while along this mountainous wall, looking for a ledge to pull myself up on, but find no way up. Finally I stop walking. A mountain like this is insurmountable. I can't climb it. Far too steep. I'm so tired. It was all for nothing, the walking, the courage I summoned. My legs give way. I slide my back down the rock, rest my head on my knees and fight back the tears. I feel my stone teardrop between my fingers. It calms me. Grandma wouldn't give up so easily. So I stand up again and continue walking, one hand on the stone. Before long, I find a narrow gap. I hear a strange rustling within. Other noises too, when I listen closely. Like a distant screeching. An echo, perhaps.

I press my face into the hole and peer inside: a path leads through it and widens out further on. I have to breathe in, suck in my belly and squeeze through the opening. I soon get the feeling I'm stuck in a rock canal. I push through. The buttons tear from my jacket and fall to the floor beneath me. Dark gleaming buttons, like a teddy bear's eyes. I press on, grazing the backs of my hands. I make it. I'm through. A narrow path leads deeper into the mountains. I take it.

The noises grow louder. There are definite cries among the rustling. But there's nothing to the left or right. I look up. Above me, strange creatures with leathery wings flap around the ravine. They look a little like featherless prehistoric birds but without the dinosaurs' pointed beaks. Their noses are rounded like a bat's, the heads too. Wide mouths with pink edges. Pointy teeth. Winged beasts, slamming into the stone walls, injuring themselves. I see their bodies flapping helplessly backwards and forwards, lurching full-speed between the rocky masses. They're incapable of escape. The cries are coming from them.

I'm standing far beneath them in the narrow ravine. Above me, the rusty-red stone walls, and between them, just a thin sliver of blue. Only visible if you crane your head backwards. The narrow path leading through the mountains is steep. Boulder after boulder to clamber over, easy to miss my footing. Some of the creatures fall down, injured; they lie briefly on the floor of the gorge, then leap back up into the air, flapping their wings, before once again crashing back down to earth.

'It's that way,' I call. My voice bounces back at me off the rock walls. Distorted. I hardly recognise my own voice. 'Look, it's that way! You have to fly higher!'

They cock their heads slightly as if hearing some distant sound and throw themselves into the rocks at breakneck speed again.

'It's that way! Just look! The sky's above you, blue sky. Just look!' I roar at the top of my lungs. But they just turn their heads helplessly, searching for the sound of my voice. It dawns on me: they're blind. They can't see me, or the walls, or the sky. And I think to myself, bats can still do it, bats can find their way in the dark. Why can't they? Their piercing shrieks are utterly pointless. All in vain. They don't prevent anything.

On the narrow path in the ravine where I'm standing lie fragments of bloody, torn-off talons. I look for one that hasn't lost its shape, a light brown, horn-like material that blends to an ebony black at the sharp tip. I pick it up, clean

off the dirt, wipe off the blood and thrust it into my jacket
pocket. Hold it tightly in my fist as I make my way through
the ravine, the edges sharp and scratchy. To remind myself
how important it is to keep searching for a way out: if you
don't look, you'll never find it.

Markus has called. For the third time. I'm a little bit
pleased about it, but I never call back. I can't right now.
I've tried to write him a letter. No success. What should
I tell him? That everyone here's gone mad?

Grandma has called too. She never does that. Dad charged
downstairs to the telephone. I ran down after him.
Listened in. But all he did was sigh.

19

I have this awful feeling that everything's still how it was two weeks ago and yet completely different. We just haven't noticed it yet. The thing we all fear still hasn't happened. And I can't do anything. Just watch on dumbly.

Rami still hasn't worked anything out. I let him into my bed today. He's so anxious, he clung to me immediately. He trembled. I cover him with my blanket, my bum and legs sticking out. He warms his icy feet on my legs. When he closes his eyes, he has incredibly long eyelashes, like a beautiful cherub.

'I'll look after you,' I say to him, once he's asleep. 'Don't be scared, my man of the house.'

Everyone's done in, except for Amina. She seems to have come alive. I'm surrounded by absolute lunatics. Ms Wischmann tells me I need to look after myself. As there's nobody else to do it.

I wait two whole flipping days. Two days of chaos and fear. And then I'm done. 'Dad,' I say. 'You can't all just keep up this silence.'

I've already been through this once with him, before, when Ms Wischmann suggested the meeting. It worked back then. Only ... back then sounds like such a long time ago. Another world, when a meeting with Ms Wischmann was possible. A world that seemed so broken at the time and yet so much better than my current one.

'Please, Dad. Mum said you want to leave. I've heard you arguing. What's wrong?'

He looks at me. Then he hugs me. I pull back momentarily. It's been so long since he last did that. Dad-smell with stale smoke in his clothes.

'Madina,' he says. 'I can't change it. And I don't want to talk about it. I can't. Do you understand?'

'I don't understand anything,' I say, holding back the tears. 'It was all going so well! We were all so happy! We got the decision, Dad. We can move out soon. Laura's mum'll help us find a place. We have everything we wanted. Why are you doing this now?'

Dad shakes his head. A gentle expression comes over his face, the one where he wants to show me or Rami that he loves us. 'I have to go back. Grandma needs me. When you grow up, you'll understand.'

'I'm already grown-up, Dad. I don't understand you all. I don't get it!'

'They've taken Uncle Miro,' says Dad.

I suddenly feel ill. 'Is he dead?' I ask. *Taken*. That usually means dead. Either straight away or in the end. 'But why do you have to leave?'

'Because without him, your grandma won't survive. Because ...'

I clamp myself onto his arm. 'Will you come back, Dad?' I ask. 'Will you get Grandma and come back?'

He sighs. And he won't look at me any more. He says softly, 'They want me to give myself up. Then they'll let him go.'

Going back means death, I reckon.

I rummage around in Dad's things and find Grandma's letter. I'm terrified about reading it, scared they'll catch me as I'm secretly hunting around Dad's bed and through his shirts and suitcase. It's so rare to find the room empty – a proper stroke of luck. Good luck within back luck. I find the letter in his things. Neatly folded. Take it with me into the toilets. Grandma's writing is spidery; it's difficult to read.

Dearest and eldest son, it begins. Between the lines large, blue splodges as if she'd been crying over the paper, or my father was, I'm not sure which.

I can't cry. I feel completely dead. I sit with my trousers around my ankles on the cold toilet, the letter in my hands, holding it close to my face to decipher it more easily.

She writes that the soldiers came. She writes that they knocked her to the floor, she's black and blue but thank God she hasn't broken anything. I think of my sweet little grandma, her flowery walls, her smile, and I can't bear to imagine coarse soldiers grabbing her and knocking her over while she whimpered with fear. That image stays with me as I read to the end of the letter.

Every sentence brings new horror. They seized my uncle, stuffed a sack over his head, pummelled him to the floor with the barrels of their guns and beat him while she lay on the floor, screaming and crying. And they laughed, and told her that her eldest son, the traitor to the people, should kindly return. And finally accept his due punishment. Her younger son would then be released. A life for a life. An eye for an eye. A tooth for a tooth.

A week has passed already, she continues. They can barely look after themselves. Grandpa is very ill; he can't take much more. They hardly dare ask, but he is the eldest son, after all, and he's responsible for all of them. She wants to know if he can return to save his younger brother. She's waiting for him. She's waiting.

No, I think to myself. It never ends. The war never ends. Once it's begun, it goes on and on, even when you're thousands of miles away. It reaches you everywhere. I think of the faces of the people on the TV, their faces distorted in horror, those who were injured in the bomb attack or were simply witnesses to the bloodbath. The violence never stops, it expands, like the ripples on the water when you toss in a pebble.

Some things happen that mean you can never return to normal. This here is one of them. I grab my school bag, ram in clean underwear for tomorrow and run away.

'Where are you going?' Mum shouts after me. She even runs after me, as far as the front gate.

'I have to see Laura,' I say.

'Come back soon!' It's not an order, more of a pleading request. She doesn't stop me. She knows there's no point.

I nod and carry on. Crossing the wood by night on foot. The real one, not my fairy tale. I've been here many times. My fear's been somewhat desensitised, like a bruised knee that no longer hurts a few days later; it just lets you know it's there and not fully healed. But I don't care. I clench my teeth and keep going. The odd car passes me, the lights like searching fingers between the branches, from the tarmac of the street. It takes a while to reach Laura's house. Her bedroom window is dark. But there's a light on downstairs. I ring the bell. I wait an absolute age and try not to think about what'll happen if Laura's not even there. Nothing moves. I call her name a few times. Then I climb over the fence, ripping a hole in my shirt, and wait for her on the patio. In the garden my father regularly tended. And soon perhaps, never again.

I waited there for hours. Cold. Hungry. I sat on the garden swing, cocooned in Laura's mum's blanket. The swing creeking. The sky was so dark, no moon, no stars. At first, the neighbour's dog kept barking. After a while he gave it up. Sometime later, Laura's mum's car pulled up, gravel spraying out from under the tyres. I heard laughter, Laura and her mum. They came into the garden.

'Hey! Someone's there,' Laura's mum said.

'Madina?' Laura asked incredulously. 'What are you doing here? Come inside, quickly, come in.' She hugged me, belly to belly, cheek to cheek. I felt numb all over. 'You're all clammy, like a salamander,' said Laura. We went inside.

The light was on because of Markus. He'd spent the whole evening listening to music through his headphones. He feels awful because I got so cold outside. He's just brought me a blanket and tea with honey, constantly apologising. I'd love to lean against him. But I daren't.

I tell them everything. Everything. They sit and listen.

'Shit,' says Markus.

'Shall I fetch Mum?' Laura asks once I'm done.

I'm not sure. It'd be good, really, if an adult was involved. I don't know how to go on alone any more.

And I tell them everything from back then. About Dad's patients. About our escape. About waiting for our leave to remain. About my uncle and my grandma and my dad who very seriously plans to save them. At the same time, I begin to cry because of course I don't want my grandma to die, or my uncle, or grandfather. The second time through is even more monstrous than the first. And Laura's mum frowns. She thinks hard.

Then she says, 'But you fled because of your dad. If your dad leaves, you have no reason to claim asylum any more. You'll have to leave too.'

It's the middle of the night and I'm sitting in Laura's mum's car. We're driving back to the boarding house.

I have to discuss this with my parents right now. Perhaps they haven't grasped that. Laura's mum's right. Dad's putting us all in danger.

Pointless to write it all down. Laura's mum, exhausted, her smeared blue eyelids drooping, and my mum, her eyes red from crying, debate across the table. I interpret everything. Amina sits to one side. Rami clings to Mum even though he's so sleepy he can barely stand.

'If you go, your family lose their right for asylum.' Laura's mum keeps banging her hand on the table. 'If you go, nobody else will believe you're in danger back home. Your whole family will have to go back! Your children will have to go back! Do you understand?'

Dad says nothing, except for, 'Do what you want. How can I let my mother, father and brother die?' He repeats it over and over.

Laura's mum looks helpless. What else can she say? She can't save Grandma, Grandpa and my uncle.

I feel like an acrobat constantly springing from one burning rope to the next. I'm bending over backwards for everyone. I just don't see why Dad can't.

'You have to get help,' says Laura's mum.

'Where from?' asks Mum.

'No idea,' says Laura's mum. 'Go to the authorities who are handling your case. You have a caseworker there, don't you? You *do* want to stay here, don't you?'

'Yes, but . . .'

I could shoot them all for this, 'Yes, but . . .'

'I want to stay here,' I cry. Now that the biggest shock has passed, it's dawned on me that they could come for me, bung me in a car and take me away, like others who have had to leave. And I'd cry and scream, and it'd all be futile. And I'd never see Laura again. Or Markus.

That makes my heart ache. I'd never see Markus again, and Dad would disappear anyway.

Laura's mum leaves and promises to call school tomorrow. She's just as confused as me. She doesn't understand it all and is clueless about Mum and Dad's lives.

I get it. It's very, very complicated. And I don't know if there's a solution.

I sit in the hallway and look out of the window. Just like my aunt, the bad role model. I gaze out at the wood, now simply an impenetrable mass with a jagged surface, over which the stars slowly begin to appear. And I wonder what Amina thinks about as she sits there, staring out like this. About her husband. About everything she's lost. About her past that she still clings to. About the things she doesn't want to let go. I understand her now. When you stop thinking about those who are gone, they disappear. As if they'd never existed. I'm responsible for Grandma, for thinking about her. And about Grandpa. And about my uncle. Even if they're not here. He was fun. He could ride horses well. He always laughed loudly.

If Dad doesn't go back, Grandma will die. If Dad does go back, he will die.

Tonight I walk through a dark valley. The sky is black. No stars, no moon. The gravel I walk on is formed of small, black,

flat pebbles, glistening. They get in my shoes, rubbing between the sole of my foot and the insole of my shoe. No wind. No noise. I'm all alone. In the distance, the sky glows. Like the glow in the sky when we left. Burning houses, burning barns. I move towards this light, frightened that I'll return to the exact same spot from which we fled. Back to the war. This journey ought to be leading me home. But to the home I had before all this began. To my real home. My childhood.

I turn around to go back. In the darkness, my feet step into emptiness. Small stones trickle away. The path I walked along has disappeared. I can't see anything. There's nothing. Not even the ground on which to tread. It's all gone. I have no choice. I have to keep going forwards. Behind me, everything has been erased. Calmly and quietly, without warning. Right. So I'll keep pushing onwards. I start to sing, to fill the void with my voice, if nothing else. I sing whatever springs to mind. Songs from my childhood. Laura's favourite songs.

The source of light draws closer and closer. The light leaps across the mountainsides, casting strange shadows like giant prehistoric animals. It gets brighter, and hotter, too. Like the wind in the desert. And a humming. A thunder-like rumble. Before me now, the footpath ends, as if simply sliced off by a huge knife. Right in the middle. In front of me gapes a chasm. And from the chasm rise two enormous, terrifying heads. Monstrous skulls, like the plastic lions they have in the Chinese restaurant in the village. Flames instead of manes. Rolling, glowing lava eyes. A taut rope divides them. As they exhale, it glows and gleams. They sit facing one another on either side of the rope, like two great watchdogs. Never letting the other out of sight. Paws raised. Matt black claws. They'd attack each other if they could. The rope keeps them apart. If only they could get close enough. They roar in pain. They're so engrossed in each other, they take no notice of me. I stay where I am. Remove my shoes and socks, stuff them into my rucksack. Wriggle my toes and mount the rope. It hurts. It burns. I take the first step. The rope wobbles and shakes.

I walk slowly, arms outstretched, step by step. My skin glows. One of the animals lets out a deafening roar, the rope sways in the draught. I lose my balance, lean to one side, dig my toes into the glowing rope. My shoes fall out of the rucksack and disappear into the depths below. I have to go on. When I finally reach the other side, the soles of my feet are smoking. I throw myself on the ground and cry from the pain.

In the middle of the night, I run to the toilet and throw up. Immediately afterwards, I'm struck down by diarrhoea. I wish for a hand to hold my head and wish this hand belonged to Laura or Markus. It feels like my confidence is pouring out of me. Top and bottom. It smells acidic. My head is spinning but don't want to ask anyone for help. I kneel on all fours in front of the toilet and fixate on the tiles. Red-brown slabs. On the left in the corner, there's a white one where something's been mended. I'll make it alone. Even if I have to crawl along the hallway back to my bedroom and into bed.

Early next morning, I call Ms Wischmann and arrange an appointment. She notes it down as an emergency and squeezes me in. Her office is far away so Laura's mum will pick me up after school and drive me there.

Mrs King brings me something sweet, to comfort me. I open it carefully – shortbread, of course. And mandarins. She means well.

At breaktime, I'm so nervous, I scratch my arm until it bleeds.

'Stop it,' says Laura quietly. 'Stop it!' And she holds me tightly, caressing me. Almost in tears herself. 'We'll work something out. Something will come up. It will.'

I waver between wanting to find something for me and the fear of betraying my family.

Markus comes to pick me up after school with Laura's mum. Watches out for me at the school gate. Takes my rucksack. It's really kind that he wants to carry it for me. Laura pulls herself together and says nothing. Doesn't look angry. We've no time for such stupidities.

On the way there, I look out the window. Look at the trees whizzing past. Count them. Even before I get to ten, I'm imagining the moss-covered trees in my wood where it's always a little bit shady, even when the suns shines. And a little hazy. I drift into my wood so easily that I only realise we're there when Markus taps me on the shoulder.

Laura's mum brings me back to the hostel. I go through all the points that Ms Wischmann has drummed into me. In my skirt pocket, there's a folded sheet of notepaper on which I've written everything in case I can't remember it all. I count the points and run my fingers over the surface of the note, as if the suggestions are written in Braille.

Markus wants to come with me. I wonder how Dad would react. I don't want to find out. I ask Laura's mum to pull over shortly before the house. Better to walk the last bit. So nobody sees he's sitting next to me in the car. Nobody else needs to know except for me. The side of my body closest to him in the car is still glowing.

It's impossibly loud in the dining room. Everyone's shouting over each other, rattling the plates and glasses. The sounds and smells assault me all at once. The revolting canteen smell. All you can hear is snippets of conversation and I just want to talk to Dad. Hear his voice, his words, and commit them to memory. Maybe they'll fragment and I'll never hear him again. And I'll wonder later, in a year's time, what he sounded like.

I have to find a reason for us to stay. If Dad leaves, then Dad's problem is no longer a reason. In the eyes of the authorities, his problem has been resolved. Why would he want to return voluntarily to a country where his life is in danger? No normal person would do such a thing. Indeed. I see those faces before me. Hard looks, pursed lips, combed hair, smart clothes. Shirts, ties. Discreet make-up or none at all. And then their critical gaze. Always the mistrustful expressions, constantly seeking out our imperfections, our insincerities, and condemning us for them. Their unspoken suspicions about why we're so desperate to stay. The only other reason we have is Amina. Whose life is in danger. But Amina would rather die than tell them anything. Or us. But if we have no grounds to stay, we'll all be deported.

I draw Dad. In case he actually goes. Then I'll have to remember what he looks like. I'll have to preserve his image within me. My drawing's bloody awful. With the dodgy moustache I've given him he starts to look like Captain Haddock. But as I add a few hairs sprouting from his chin, he becomes more like Hagrid. I'll take a photo. Somehow.

What do you do when you're powerless to do anything? Crying doesn't help. I'll just somehow carry on until I think of something.

I've made it. I can hardly believe it. I've dodged all the terrible animals in my wood. Defeated the mist fields. Trekked through the mountains. I'm so close to my goal. My feet are scratched and bleeding. But I'm happy. All that remains is the final descent to the sand. Across the dunes to the sea. There's a jetty. I know it. I've been there before. And there, waiting at the jetty is my ship. Waiting at anchor the whole time. For me alone. The captain can navigate the star-studded night sky far better than me. He has a brass telescope that guides him, and star charts and lunar calendars, he knows the tides and the patterns of the waves. He knows everything we need for our crossing. And he's waiting for me. Waiting for me, just like the sailors, whose only reason for being there is to maintain this ship and carry out his orders.

I run, I stumble, the sand getting into the wounds between my toes, into my clothes. It's warm. Very fine grains. I protect my eyes with my hand and see the sea beyond. There. That's it. I can make out the outline of the ship. I laugh, fall to my knees in the sand and laugh, throwing my head back, until I can't breathe. I stand up again and set off at a run.

It's an old ship with a huge blue sail and creaky boards. But as I reach the dock and try to go aboard, they block my way.

'Hey!' I shout. 'It's taken me weeks to get to you. What's all this about?'

A sailor leans over the side and calls back, 'This is your only way, what can you pay with? We're setting sail today.'

I drop my hands.

'I have nothing,' I say.

'Then you'll have to stay here,' he replies.

My legs buckle. It can't all have been in vain. All of this. It can't be. I won't allow it. I rummage through my pockets. Nothing in the first one. Not even a morsel to eat. In the second one, I prick my forefinger on something sharp. I pull out the bloodied horn talon I picked up in the ravine. 'Look!' I shout. 'I can give you this.'

'Wait there,' the sailor calls back and disappears.

I stand there, my eyes drifting out to sea. I have to cross to the other side. I have to get to Grandma.

After a while, the sailor reappears with a tall man. Dark shirt and dark circles under his eyes. Blue eyes. Beard like Dad. Somehow looks like Dad. That suddenly throws me. I don't want any likenesses here, in my world.

They heave a plank over the side and it thuds down onto the dock. The man climbs slowly down towards me. Takes the piece of horn and weighs it in his hand. The palm of his hand is huge compared to mine, covered with calluses and dark like the corroded railings. He smells of the sea and spices.

'OK,' he says. 'I'll take it.'

I start towards the plank. He bars my path.

'What now?' I ask. 'I've paid for my crossing.'

'That's not enough,' he says.

'I have nothing else,' I stutter.

He points to the teardrop hanging around my neck and says, 'That'll do.'

I swallow. The teardrop has led me this far. What will I do without it? But I must keep going. I can't go back. I take a deep breath, pull off the chain I've been wearing round my neck since I left home, yank it downwards and place the silver jewel in his paw.

He laughs and closes his finger. The sparkle disappears into his fist.

'Welcome aboard,' he says, turning around and climbing up.

I follow him up the wobbly, narrow plank.

I'm on the phone, listening to the beeps. A notebook in front of me in which I've written the most important points. I'm waiting endlessly in a queue. As the female voice answers, I'm so distracted, I forget to speak straight away.

'Who is it?'

'Madina. Eli's daughter.'

'Eli who? Madina who?'

I give our surname. Our case number.

'Yes?'

'Can I come over with my mother?'

'Why?'

'We need a separate appointment. I need help.'

'What do you need?' The voice sounds disbelieving.

'Help and an appointment. It's urgent!'

'First appointment in two weeks.'

'Yes, OK.'

She hangs up before I have time to thank her.

I'm scared I'll forget something important. I'm scared I won't remember what he looks like. I lie there every night piecing together his face. The eyes. The eyebrows. The scar on his chin, there's a small bald patch in his beard. I miss something every time. How will I do it when I no longer see him every day? The parts I can't remember, they're gone. Lost. Perhaps for ever.

Markus wanted to come and visit. I've said no. Not now.

Dad's started packing. I can't believe it. I simply cannot believe it. But he's serious. He's leaving us. He's leaving me.

20

Dad's been playing badminton with Rami in the yard this evening after dinner. I've been watching. Too tired to run around. I want to write to Grandma. But I don't know what to write. I hold the piece of paper and fold it into different shapes. Should I write something like, *Please stay alive? Please.*

Feel empty. Watch the white shuttlecock fly up. The sound of the rubber tip as it meets the racket, and the whirring as it whizzes through the air. A monotonous to and fro. Toss up, hit, fly. Over and over. Rami's more agile than Dad, quicker too. Gets to every shot and Dad loses hands down. He pants. Holds his chest as he does whenever he's exerted himself. Before, when I'd see him clutch his chest like that, I'd feel uneasy.

Rami performs a celebratory dance, like he's forgotten what's going on. Dad grabs hold of him and hugs him. Their sweaty T-shirts stick to their bodies. The wisteria shimmers violet against the crumbling render of the building walls. The sky is still light and the fat mayflies hum in the air like small, slow, bronze bullets. It smells like the start of summer. Like the start of something good. I know it's a lie.

Laura visits and tries to cheer us up. Tells me that Markus really wants to see me. Wants to do something for me. That's kind. But other than sitting with me, there's nothing he can do. Sometimes there's nothing else to do other than sit patiently next to someone. Like I used to do with the patients in our cellar. If I had to choose right now what I want to be when I'm older, I've definitely decided. Even if Mrs King thinks I'm unsuitable for it. I still want to be a doctor.

Laura promises Rami that he'll get a rabbit if he's good and tries not to be sad. Her neighbour is giving some away.

'Really?' Rami's face lights up. 'I'd like one with black and white spots.'

'Come over and have a look,' Laura tempts him. 'Madina will come too, won't you, Madina?'

During the night, Mum and Dad unwittingly stage another radio play for me. They think I'm asleep like Rami. I'm lying here, breathing steadily so they don't realise. I hate eavesdropping but I have to know what's going on. So I can make my own plans.

Dad: Sleep now. The children need you.

Mum: They need you, too.

DAD: I'll come back.

MUM: Do you really believe that? I don't.

DAD: I have to believe it. How else can I leave? Perhaps it'll all be fine. Miracles can happen. Miracles *do* happen. Sometimes. Why not? This is a safe country, cocooned in a snow globe where it always snows ... We have a chance! We could free ourselves. With money. I'll write a letter. I'll promise to return ... And offer them a deal. I'll pay a ransom. Then my brother goes free and we all escape.

MUM: But we've got nothing.

DAD: I'll borrow something.

MUM: How's that going to work?

DAD: Everyone's open to bribery.

MUM: They'll take our money and you two as well! That's what'll happen. We both know it.

DAD: I'll come back and bring my brother and parents with me. It'll be tough. But I know the way. I know the way.

MUM: You're just saying that to reassure me ... I've had it with moving. I've moved enough for a whole lifetime. God, I long for peace and quiet ...

DAD: Sleep now. I'll still be here in the morning.

And I lie there and know the only person left who can do anything now is me. Me alone. Well, OK, not completely. And Laura. And Ms Wischmann. I think about her double chin and her colourful earrings, think

261

how grateful I am to her. Feel my arms and legs getting
really heavy.

*That night I lie on deck and stare up into the expansive night
sky. The stars are huge, so big you feel you could touch them.
I count shooting stars like other people count sheep when they
can't sleep. They leave a silvery trail against the velvety blue
sky.*

*The night is silent. All day long seagulls cry as they
accompany us, waiting for the fish the sailors throw to them.
The seagulls are our protectors, they tell me. Mermaids don't
like seagulls. And the seamen don't like mermaids. They're too
dangerous. Sometimes we see dragonfish in the distance, their
shimmering red backs breaking the water's surface. Gleaming
manes and sharp spines. They grow to over fifteen metres long
and when they catch a human in the water, they coil themselves
in golden loops around their victim and drag them down into
the depths. That's why I never go in the water. The seagulls'
cries mimic human voices when they're hungry.*

*At night-time, we're followed by shoals of silvery discus
fish and mermaids who lure the sailors. They have golden
hair and gilded combs, such beautiful faces, and soft, webbed
hands. Their scaly skin is pale and shimmering. Their top
halves as light as mother of pearl, their tails green with a hint
of blue, blue-green like the sea itself when it's light and
friendly, and the sun shines.*

'Just look how beautiful they are!' I call.

'Don't look at them for too long,' says one of the sailors, who's just clambered down the mast. He has suntanned arms and white trousers. Wide harem pants that remind me of One Thousand and One Nights. *Dark brown eyes. I'm certain I've seen someone like that on TV.* 'Don't look at them, or you'll go overboard.'

I curl my fingers around the railing. I must not fall in the water. I still have to get home. I have to find the way home, to Grandma. I close my eyes. But I can still hear them. As they laugh and call. Their voices, however, aren't beautiful.

We ignore them, don't respond and avoid the cliff-edge where they have positioned themselves like customs officers collecting a toll as you cross their border. As we travel past, their voices suddenly turn animalistic and threatening. They cackle and sing songs to provoke bad weather. The clouds quickly gather above us and the sea changes colour: from turquoise blue to dark grey. Waves crash. In the storm, the water nymphs' scales change too. Become dull and leaden. Their eyes lose their sparkle. Their skin takes on a grey hue with blue shadows on their shoulders and throat. Only their blood-red mouths retain any colour. As they rise from the water near the keel, they shriek, stretching their hands out towards us – I see their silver, razor-sharp claws. The foam sprays up towards the railing, I shrink backwards. Behind me the mast creaks, the wind whistles in the rigging above me. Their laughter accompanies our ship long after we sail past. I'm pleased not

*to be alone, to be protected. This team is a loyal community
that understands the ship far better than I. I can rely on them.*

I find a piece of paper on which Dad's clearly been making
notes. Notes about the things he needs to pack, telephone
numbers of people who could take him; he can't afford
a plane ticket, not even a train. *Take chewing gum* is
there. A book he wants to read on the way. Photos of me
and Rami. And right at the bottom he's written: *There is
no way out . . . only violence. Violence everywhere. If I stay
here: violence. If I don't stay here: violence. How can I
resolve it?*

I'd love to know who he's asking. Himself? Or some
higher power?

At breaktime I sit with Laura in the toilets and sob out
all the bodily fluids I possess. She holds me tight and
cries with me.

Ms Wischmann's coming to my appointment with the
caseworker. Said she wants to get informed. She's promised
she'll come. Without her, I'd easily mess it all up.

Dad's started all this *Head of the Family* nonsense again. Although I get the feeling nobody really believes him any more, not even Rami.

When I go somewhere official with Ms Wischmann, I'm treated really differently. I go in and there's someone with me who's there just for me. It feels all brand new. If it wasn't all so awful, I'd be really pleased about it. They smile as we enter the room. Everyone we met today did, anyway. No mistrustful sign already painted on the threshold. Ms Wischmann asks question after question. I simply have to listen. For the first time, just sit and do nothing. The authorities are forced to discuss our case significantly more than usual. Ms Wischmann arranges the next appointment. For two days' time.

When Dad goes, I'm the only one here who knows what we have to do. I know because I've talked to the authorities, and Crowface, and Ms Wischmann, and Laura's mum. And Mr Bast. And with the school nurse. OK, I only saw the school nurse because I was still trembling. But I'm starting to feel calmer. I know which authorities are responsible for us. I know which decision-makers – that's what they call them here – we have to talk to. I know how to get there. I know what we have to tell them and how. Mum's never been. Mum has no idea. She needs all her energy to say goodbye to Dad and to comfort Rami. She has nothing left over. Of all people, the only one who can help me is Amina, who perhaps wants to go back even less than I do. Amina could be the key to a firmly locked door, behind which the solution is waiting. But it won't be easy.

Dad's bag is packed and ready behind the door. Been there for several days. But he's still here. Waiting for the chance to travel with others. Sits waiting at the table for the call. Dad on standby.

Mum's progressed to acting out some absurd kind of everyday life. Like a show. I play along because not playing along means being completely shut out. And I imagine us staying here alone and don't want any regrets afterwards.

Went to Laura's this afternoon. We watched some rubbish TV series. Six episodes one after the other. And stuffed in one chocolate after the other, too.

So. Dad's call came in. He's off the day after tomorrow. I can't hug him, even though I want to. I know I should. I know I might never see him again. But I can't.

Should be at school tomorrow. Called in absent. Mrs King has authorised it.

I'm tossing and turning in bed. I toss and turn so long it feels like the mattress is swaying beneath me. And soon I can hear the creaking of the wooden planks I'm lying on. Stretch my hand away from the mattress onto the floor and know it's no longer plastic laminate but real, rough wood with cracks I can run my fingers along. No longer a bedroom floor but the ship's deck.

The ship moves beneath me and beneath the ship moves the sea. The wind beats my face. It hurts a little. It's raining. Water above and below. It's not yet night but the sky is dark. The clouds gathering above the ship are almost black. A dark wall that suddenly extends. Every so often the sky lights up. Rumbles of thunder. I taste the salt on my lips.

'Don't worry, it'll blow over,' I tell myself, as my father used to do.

Sailors run past me. One shouts, 'Hurry! Hurry!'

The mast groans. Waves grow higher and higher, a torrent of water crashes overboard. The ship's bow drops, falling, my stomach heaves and I look for something to hold on to. If the next wave takes me, I'll be washed overboard and I know nobody will notice. A box flies past me. On the box perches a cat. She has no fear. Since when are there cats on ships? I lose my balance, trip and fall to my knees, pull myself up and run again towards the others, where, in the middle of the haze, hangs a light. A lamp.

'Trust yourself,' says a familiar voice. Someone's said that to me before . . .

A flash of lightning. Blinded, I briefly close my eyes. As the thunder begins, I open them again. I'm standing on the bridge. I look around for the captain. There's nobody else but me. The huge, old wheel spins without a steersman. I scream. Nobody replies. In the pouring rain I can see neither captain nor sailors, I'm completely alone.

I realise whose voice it was: Ms Wischmann.

The ship lurches again, I fight against gravity. Grab the wheel, hold on tight. Press my body against it to make it turn. Scream with anger and fear, scream from effort. Throw my full weight and energy against the wooden wheel. As I press even more, it gives. I keep going. I cling to the wheel. I'm thrown to and fro. I don't let go. Not until I see the ship turning as I want it to, until it's on course. I stand on the bridge, wheel in my hands. Above me I hear the sirens' song but I can't see any of them. I know what they look like: feathered arms, naked breasts, red lips, loose hair blowing in the wind. I pay them no attention. I have a ship to steer. The wheel is in my hands, it acts under my will. I feel the power of the ship combining with the power of the sea. I am the helmswoman.

When I wake up, I know what I have to do.

21

In the morning, I walk over to Amina who has already taken up her early morning position at the window. I plant myself behind her and try to make myself look imposing, invincible. I've practised in the mirror. For hours. Studied the sheet that Ms Wischmann gave me, going through everything we wrote down point by point. When I climb up on this wire rope and take the first step, I can't afford to hesitate or glance down, otherwise I'll lose my balance and we'll all come crashing down.

'Amina,' I say. 'It's about survival.'

She smiles. 'Isn't it always about survival?' she asks.

'Usually,' I reply.

'But not everyone makes it,' she says.

'I know,' I say. 'But in our case, we have to succeed. It'll be the end of all of us if we have to go back.'

Even she looks horrified.

And I say, 'I know you're scared, Amina. I'm scared too.'

She turns to face me and, for once, doesn't look cross.

'I know how we can avoid it,' I say. 'But we have to do it right. We have to try.'

'What do you mean?' she asks cautiously.

'You have to tell them what happened to you.'

She pushes me away. I try to retain my balance.

'Never, never,' she squeezes out between her teeth. 'I haven't told anyone and I never will.'

I stay rooted where I am. Close to her. I say it as quietly as possible. 'Well then, Amina, they'll send us back. There'll be an arrest warrant out for you. And everything that goes with it. You know that better than me, Amina.'

She draws her scarf up, around her shoulders, around her neck, even cloaking her face in it, hiding away in the shadow of her scarf, as if she could crawl away into it, veiling her from my view. But of course, I can still see her.

'I know it's really hard,' I say. 'But going back is even harder. Mum will ask your forgiveness. *I* ask your forgiveness. Whether Dad will, I don't know. But Dad's going and we want to stay here. Please, Amina.'

She lifts her head and gives me a piercing look.

'We want to do it differently. I want to do it differently,' I say.

She laughs. I don't.

'What's going to change?' she says.

'Our lives.'

'A-ha. Really?'

'They've already changed a lot. *I've* changed a lot, look. Why not you too?'

Amina bares her teeth at me again, complete with missing tooth.

If I tried to touch her now, she'd snap at me like a wild animal. But I don't touch her, instead I steal closer. She's uneasy. But she doesn't pull away.

'Why would they believe me?'

'They believed Dad.'

'You don't know that.'

'I do,' I say emphatically. 'I was there.'

'He's a man.' It comes out as a hiss.

'Women are treated differently here. Better.'

Amina scrutinises me.

She thinks.

'Think about Laura's mum,' I say. 'Think about my teacher. Think about Ms Wischmann. They live alone. They live differently.'

'Are they happy?'

'I don't know. But they do what they think is right.'

'If they laugh at me, I will never forget it,' she says. And I sense she's already relented.

I'll go the whole hog today, while I have the energy to do so. You have to use your energy when you have it. Rest when you can't go on. And then just get back up again and keep on going. That's what Dad's taught me.

I rummage around in the wardrobe drawers until I find the scissors. I'll need them later.

Mum's out. That's unusual because she's usually always here. I look for her on the first, then second, then third floor. I even look for her in the bosses' flat. I don't give up. I walk down every single hallway, rattle every bathroom and toilet door handle. On the second floor, I hear snuffling behind one of the toilet doors. Softly. I knock. The snuffling suddenly stops. She's petrified.

'Mum,' I call. 'It's me, Madina. Are you in there? Open the door. Please.'

She sniffs and fiddles with the catch. It takes a while because she can't get it at first. She opens the door a crack. 'Come in,' she whispers.

I slide through the gap. She's crouching in the corner on the floor, on the cold tiles. She's banned me from doing that. So I don't get a urine infection. I can't sit next to her because the cubicle is too narrow. I squeeze in, close the toilet lid, sit on it and pull my knees up to my chin. We're silent for a moment. I want to give her time.

'Mum,' I say finally. 'You know we have to do something.'

She sobs. I let her cry, wait a while, and start again.

'Mum, we have to think of something.'

She looks at me. Her gaze is so empty it's as if Mum isn't in there any more. Just a skin and a lot of water.

I think of Rami. I think of me. I won't give up. For the me that's lived here and no longer has a place back home.

'Mum,' I say. 'I want to live here. I want to live. You know that.'

And she nods and cries even more.

'You have to fill out your own application,' I say. 'I'm still a minor, I can't do it. But you can.'

She continues looking at me silently. Quizzically.

'You can do it,' I repeat. My voice doesn't tremble. 'I'll do it with you, Mum. With Rami. And with Amina. Amina has to testify. Amina *has* to explain what happened to her and her husband. And you have to confirm it. But *you* have to do something. You have to stand up and you have to do it.'

She keeps staring dead ahead. Her silence makes me so incredibly nervous, but I pretend not to be. Hide my hands in my sweatshirt pocket so Mum can't see my fingers tapping on the back of my hand. 'Mum,' I say a bit louder. 'Do you love me? If you do, you'll do this.'

And she nods, nodding eagerly like a schoolgirl, and rubs her eyes, nose, mouth with her hand, as if trying to rub away her whole face. Roughly. And she gives me a lopsided smile. 'Yes, I do.'

Even though it's anything but funny, I almost laugh because it sounds so similar to a marriage vow.

'That's good, Mum,' I say. 'Then we'll go tomorrow.'

Tonight I'm running full pelt back through my journey. Through the wood. Past the animals. Across the mist fields. Along the ravine. Through the abyss. I know the way, I mustn't stop moving. To the ship. Ignore the sirens and cross the sea. Can't see the country I'm steering towards because it's night-time and dark. And yet I know what it looked like as we left: layers of sand and stone, marbled like meat, with a sweet layer of grass on top like skin. The land looks as though it's been bitten off, just as I felt bitten off back then too, as we set off, as if someone had sunk their teeth into me and torn out a piece. This tearing sensation has lasted a long time. Something like that takes time to heal, scars form around the edges of the wound. Eventually, they say, you'll be able to touch it without it hurting. Without it scaring you.

Everything is the same, nothing has changed. Birds nesting on the cliffs, black swarms of little birds.

As dawn breaks, the ship docks. A jolt through the hull almost knocks me off my feet. The sea is grey. The sun is coming up. I disembark, crossing the wobbly plank I'm no longer afraid of. Everything has been swaying beneath me for so long, it feels completely normal. No longer throws me off balance. I set foot on land and know that she's there, perhaps she's been standing there the whole time. The small, plump figure with the colourful shawl around her shoulders.

'Grandma,' I cry. The wind whips my words away but she raises her head and comes towards me. I start to run; we meet in the middle. She smells musty, mixed with roses, like always. She's soft and warm, I press my cheek against the crescent of pale skin that escapes her dress. She places her shawl across my shoulders. I want to disappear inside it, be little again, so small she can wrap her arms all the way around me, light as a baby. I feel my body shrinking. My arms and legs becoming shorter, my neck, my head, small and round once again, I can barely stand. I stretch out my stubby little arms towards her and cry and laugh.

And she smiles and says, 'Well, well,' and bends over to pick me up. We snuggle into each other until my breathing calms down. And then she looks at me very seriously and says, 'You know you have to go back, don't you?'

I close my eyes. I shake my head wildly and murmur, 'Please just let me stay here.'

And she caresses me and says: 'But your place isn't here. You know that.' And she slips off her necklace, the one from which she hangs the pendant, the silver palm with the eye on it, that I gave to her as we left, and she hangs it back around my neck.

As my body begins to grow again at top speed, I wake up.

22

The birds are still asleep. I'm already awake. It's misty outside. As the sun rises, the rays sometimes appear as golden fingers grasping among the white haze on the mountainside. But still no morning light.

Before we set off for the station that morning, my father says, 'Thank you.'

I know what he means. For looking after Rami. And Mum. 'You left me no choice,' I say.

He says, 'I never had a choice.'

I walk on. Counting my steps. Counting the tree trunks to keep me from running away. There are big, strong trees here, with grey-green lichen. But none as big or as tall as the ones in my wood. Lighter. More clearings along the way. In the fairy tale of Hansel and Gretel, they left a trail of breadcrumbs. I've fed my bread straight to the birds in the tree. I'm not sorry. I have to find my own way, can't use breadcrumbs.

Mum walks a little way behind me. Not so far behind though that I feel I'm leading us as Dad led us. Behind her walks Amina. Amina's footsteps are as silent as mine. She's wearing soft-soled shoes. I imagine she can feel every root on the path under the balls of her feet. Another wanderer in the hazy wood. I can sense it. She's visited that place too, just as I have. But her creatures in the dark look different to mine, they act differently. They haven't been kind to her. Mine tolerate me. She's still there. She takes false steps in the mist fields and hears the birds crying from afar, but she can't find a way out. I can't help her; she has to do it herself.

I hear her breathing. Hear the leaves beneath Mum's shoes. The train station isn't far away. I don't like the silence but I don't know what to say. So we don't say anything. It's cool, the haze creeps up the mountainside, the landscape appears as an illusion. I imagine seeing myself from a distance, walking through the trees.

'You see, Mum?' I say.

'What?' she asks. And then she continues, 'You know the way?'

And I mumble, 'Yes. Who else?'

Is that me, I ask myself. Is that really me? Am I really taking my mother? Rather than my mother taking me? Why am I leading everyone? And then I wonder, where is she headed, this Madina who sometimes seems so alien to me? When she turns around, perhaps she'll no longer have my face. And what is she talking about? What is she wittering on about as she walks and walks? And then I hear not only my mumbling, but other voices, too. Lots of them. Distinct. They keep calling and calling. So tender, so deceitful, calling my name from afar. 'Come to us,' they cry. But I know. 'No, no, I can't follow you, if I go there, there's no way back.'

Strange, visiting the same place I visited time and again with Dad. Only this time without Dad. I know the drill. We tear off our ticket, we walk along the narrow linoleum floor. I lead the way just as I led them through the woods to the train station. Their world stops at the fence around the house. There, mine begins.

We've been appointed a different caseworker. No longer the forgettable man who Dad had to deal with. Ms Wischmann has told her everything. She's friendly. Perhaps because she thinks I'm kind. Perhaps because she knows they're keeping an eye on us. It's good to think that someone knows about us.

Someone comes for Amina. A man. Her face turns green. She's meant to go into a separate room. For questioning. She looks at me in horror.

'I want to go with her,' I say.

'That's not allowed, we have interpreters. You won't be required.'

'Yes, I will,' I say loudly and forcefully. 'She's scared. She's scared of men. She wants to talk to a woman.'

The man rolls his eyes.

I stay where I am. 'I know she has the right to talk to a woman,' I say. 'I've promised her.'

They talk among themselves. We wait for a woman.

The lady responsible for Mum and me smiles at me and places a hand on my shoulder. 'You're doing great,' she says. And adds, 'We could do with someone like you around here.'

And really, it sounds ridiculous, but I think, 'I know.'

That evening I stand in the bathroom and hold the scissors to my face. I want to change something in my life. Put everything that was, behind me. Or at least a part of it. I take a strand of hair, pull it free. Run my fingers along the long, flat surface. Wind it around my hand. A black-blue shiny bracelet. I'll miss it, this feeling under my fingertips. The compliments. Perhaps Markus likes my hair the way it is. Or perhaps even just my hair. Whatever.

When I was little, I did things to appease fate. If I give away my last lollipop, my family will be happy, I thought. Or, I'll give away my toys. As an offering. Just one more.

I raise the scissors, place the strands between the blades, test the tension and cut them with one chop. The scissors and the hair together create a strange, dull sound. It's harder than I thought. The next time I pick up less hair in one go. The strands fall in gentle spirals, landing as darks snakes around my bare feet. And the next ones. And the ones after that. After the fourth section, I feel lighter.

My hair now comes down to my chin. It looks funny. Naked. No fear now. I don't take my eyes off my face. Mr Bast told us in class that hair retains all the information about our bodies.

Happiness. Stress. Illness. For years. Away with it all.

I gather together the silky carpet of hair and stuff all of it except for one lock carelessly into the dustbin. This one I'll stick in my diary. I look again in the mirror. I look like a stranger. Run my hand through my hair. Where I used to feel resistance, my hand now pulls free. I close the door behind me. Feels good.

As I enter the room, my mum gasps. Dad looks at me. Nods. I think he understands. I hope so. Nobody says anything. We lie down silently. Lights out. In the darkness I drift as in an unknown river.

It's getting light again. Nobody goes for breakfast.

Outside, a car horn beeps. Dad stands up, sighs, shoulders his rucksack and walks to the door.

Rami runs over to him.

Mum makes no sound. If she opens her mouth now, only sobs will come out.

Rami tears the door open in front of Dad. 'I'll be waiting for you, Dad,' he says. 'When you get back, maybe I'll have a pet.'

We go down the stairs. A small, miserable procession. Dad first with his luggage, after him, Rami, then Mum, and finally me.

'Your food, Eli,' squeaks Mum and hands him a package that looks just like my school packed lunch. She holds Rami's hand. Dad hugs her, pinches Rami's cheek. He opens the front door.

From outside comes a gust of wind, blowing in leaves. He hugs me. I rest my head briefly on his shoulder. He ruffles my hair.

'Your hair will have grown out by the time I'm back,' he says.

I say nothing. I wave.

Dad waves back.

He turns around and steps outside. The door closes. *He's going.*

We're staying here.

I'm staying here.

WHY WE
TOOK THE CAR

WOLFGANG HERRNDORF

Mike doesn't get why people think he's boring. Sure, he doesn't have many friends. (OK, zero friends.) And everyone laughs at him in class. And he's never invited to parties.

But one day Tschick, the odd new boy at school, shows up at Mike's house. He dares him to go on a road trip with him. No parents, no map, no destination. Will they get hopelessly lost in the middle of nowhere? Probably. Will they get into serious trouble? Definitely. But will they ever be called boring again? Not a chance.

'You will see the world with different eyes after reading this novel'
Rolling Stone